THE ADDAMS FAMILY

THE JUNIOR NOVEL

THE ADDAMS FAMILY

THE JUNIOR NOVEL

Adapted by
CALLIOPE GLASS

HARPER
An Imprint of HarperCollinsPublishers

The Addams Family: The Junior Novel
Printed in the United States of America.
No part of this book may be used or reproduced in any manner whatsoever without written permission
except in the case of brief quotations embodied in critical articles and reviews. For information address
HarperCollins Children's Books, a division of HarperCollins Publishers,
195 Broadway, New York, NY 10007.
www.harpercollinschildrens.com
Library of Congress Control Number: 2019941734
ISBN 978-0-06-294682-9
19 20 21 22 23   PC/BRR   10 9 8 7 6 5 4 3 2 1
❖
First Edition

PROLOGUE

At the top of a jagged cliff over the churning sea, preparations were under way for a wedding.

An Addams wedding.

There were no white flowers. There was no frothy lace. The town church stood empty, and the townsfolk shivered and scowled as they watched the bride stride up the street toward the cliff. Heat lightning flickered in the darkening sky. A few bats fluttered behind the bride as she and her black-clad bridesmaids made their way up to the cliff.

"They don't belong here!" one townsperson hissed to another.

"They're frightening the children!" she replied.

"Who do they think they are?" another villager spat.

They watched as the bride and her bridesmaids disappeared into the gloomy night, vanishing into the scrub that lined the path up to the top of the cliff.

The villagers glared after them.

"They've got to go," said one, and the rest nodded.

Morticia Frump kept climbing up the hill toward the cliff that overlooked the sea. She ignored how the townsfolk whispered and pointed. She didn't care what they thought. They were boring, normal people with small minds and prejudiced hearts.

No, today Morticia had better things to think about. She was ready to get married. Not only was she marrying the man of her dreams, but the wedding would bring together two great families. The Frumps and the Addamses were the strangest folks around, and they'd always had so much in common. Morticia smiled at the thought that her wedding would unite everyone.

She'd been preparing all morning. Her knee-high boots were bolted on. Her corset was tightened to the "strangle" setting. Her nails had been dipped in molten lead for that perfect dull gray hue. And her dress looked like it had been stolen from someone's grave . . . which it very well might have been.

Morticia looked terrifying. Which was exactly how she wanted to look.

She reached the top of the hill, then paused. Here, the hill evened out into a narrow strip of level land. You could walk about ten paces before you hit the crumbling edge of the cliff. One step past that edge, and you'd plummet five hundred feet down into a churning ocean. The footing was uncertain in the dark of night. The odds that someone might wander off the edge of the cliff by accident were pretty high. It was the perfect place for a wedding.

Morticia smiled. And the collected Addams and Frump clans, gathered there at that cliff to celebrate her wedding, smiled back. There were a large number of people assembled on the narrow cliff's edge. Every single one of them was strange. Some of them were creepy. Others were kooky. One or two were altogether ooky.

And they were all of them just thrilled to be there.

Awaiting Morticia was Gomez, the groom. He sweated nervously in his funeral suit (nothing but the best for a wedding, after all). The band—a ragtag collection of organ grinders and sackbut players—began a dirge-like rendition of "Here

Comes the Bride," and Gomez snapped to attention.

Morticia was coming.

Gomez wasn't sure if he'd ever been this terrified in his life. His stomach churned. His vision swam. His knees trembled and his ears rang. It was the worst he'd ever felt. He wished he could feel like this forever.

Pat, pat. Gomez patted his pockets anxiously, checking to make sure he had the ring. *Pat, pat.*

Pat, pat.

Pat.

Patpatpatpatpat—where was the ring?! Gomez looked around frantically. Had he dropped it? Just then, a disembodied hand scampered up. It was running on its fingers like a rat scrambling along on four legs. The hand leapt into the air and snapped its fingers sharply. Gomez looked up just in time. The hand—Thing—tossed the lost ring at him, and Gomez snatched it out of the air with a flourish.

"Thanks, Thing!" he murmured.

And at that moment, Morticia appeared. All the thoughts fell out of the bottom of Gomez's brain. He just stared.

Morticia.

She looked—she looked like seventy snakes stuffed into an evening gown. She looked like someone who wouldn't think twice before running several thousand volts of direct current through your head. She looked like a hedge witch at a nightclub. She looked like bad news. She looked like the last thing you see when you die.

She looked unspeakably beautiful—scratch that; she looked *unspeakable*.

Morticia came to a stop next to Gomez. "*Cara mia,*" he murmured at her. She winked at him.

The priest stepped up, and Gomez tore his eyes away from Morticia. The wedding ceremony was beginning.

"Dearly be-loathed," the priest said, raising his arms and addressing the entire crowd. "What an honor to witness the union of these two horrible young people . . . and these two perfectly awful families!"

The crowd let out a bloodcurdling (and heartwarming) cheer.

The priest turned to Morticia.

"Do you, Morticia Frump, take Gomez Addams to have and to hurl, in sickness and depravity, until you drop dead?"

Morticia nodded eagerly.

Meanwhile, as the wedding ceremony continued, the townspeople swarmed up the hill. They'd finally had enough of the Addamses and the Frumps. They were armed with torches and ready for mob action.

"This will teach them not to blindly conform," one of them muttered as they hurried along the path up to the cliff.

The priest turned to Gomez.

"Do you, Gomez Addams—"

"Yes, yes, a thousand times yes!" Gomez interrupted him. He didn't mean to be rude—he just couldn't wait to get married! Morticia was the perfect woman. She was cold, cruel, and terrifying. Gomez clutched Morticia's hand passionately. She clutched him back, her lead-tipped fingernails digging into his hand. He winced, and shivered happily.

More and more townspeople joined the mob. Soon the crowd streaming up the hill formed a torchlit parade. They waved pitchforks, shovels, torches; several people pushed a homemade catapult.

It would have been festive if it weren't so murderous.

The priest smiled. "I now pronounce you—"

"Monsters!" A piercing scream tore through the night air.

The assembled Frumps and Addamses turned around—there, cresting the hill, was a ravening mob of small-minded townsfolk.

"Oh dear," Morticia murmured, her eyes widening. "A ravening mob of small-minded townsfolk."

Frumps and Addamses screamed and ran as the mob burst in waving torches and crude weapons. Several townsfolk were setting up the catapult and loading it with firebombs.

"Again?!" Gomez groaned.

Morticia sighed and shook her head. "Why do hordes of angry villagers follow us everywhere we go?" she said, dodging a shoe flung by an outraged farmwife. "Don't they have better things to wave pitchforks at?"

A ball of flame rocketed toward them, launched by the catapult. Gomez swept Morticia out of its path. "Perhaps we should discuss it later," he suggested. Around them, panicked family members scrambled and ran, slipping through the crowds of angry villagers and scattering into the night.

The villagers ran after them. Morticia and Gomez fled with Gomez's mother and his brother Fester. Soon they were cornered.

"I'll hold them off," Grandma Addams said, drawing

her sword. She slashed it viciously through the air, and the villagers flinched back for a moment.

"Grab on to my hairy back!" Fester cried. He tore off his shirt, and Gomez and Morticia clung to his luxurious back hair as he scrambled to safety.

Morticia felt her heart breaking.

Her perfect wedding day, ruined. A memory that should have been cherished, tarnished. A family that had come together, now scattered to the ends of the earth. Morticia *loved* chaos and anguish, sure, but on her own terms. This . . . this was just *mean*.

Normal people were not to be trusted. It only ended in fire and tears.

Gomez wrapped a comforting arm around her. "We're safe, my love," he said gently. "That's all that matters."

Morticia wiped tears away, being careful to smear her mascara and eyeliner as she did it.

"You look like a zombie raccoon now," Gomez observed admiringly.

"Oh, good," Morticia said. She already felt a little better. "But where on earth will we go?" The Frumps had been driven out of nearly every community in Western Europe by now, and the Addamses had exhausted all of Eastern Europe. There had just been *so many* pitchfork-wielding mobs over the last few centuries. Morticia thought about it. Perhaps Zanzibar? Or maybe they could try their luck in Australia.

As if sensing her line of thought, Gomez said, "We will find a *new* homeland. Somewhere exotic. Somewhere magical. Somewhere that's truly . . . *us*."

"*Oh*," Morticia breathed. "Are you thinking what I'm thinking?"

Gomez smiled back at her. "Yes, my dear. We both know where we must go."

New Jersey did not disappoint.

It was barbaric, uncultured, crass, confusing, and dirty. And it smelled bad. Everywhere.

"Unhappy, darling?" Gomez asked, catching Morticia's hand and kissing it as they tore along a country road in the dead of night. The trees were tall. The hills were rolling. The moon glinted through the dead marsh grass, where it was reflected in the fetid swamp water on either side of the road.

It smelled *terrible*. Morticia *loved* this state.

"Yes," she breathed, "I'm terribly unhappy. It's *wonderful*."

But now that the honeymoon was over . . . Morticia sighed.

"Darling," Gomez said, looking concerned. "Is that a wrinkle I see on your pallid brow? What's wrong?"

Morticia clutched his hand. Thing yanked the wheel, and the limo tore around another curve. A dense fog had suddenly gathered, shrouding the road in dark mist. It was impossible to see farther than ten feet down the road. New Jersey! What a charming place.

"We can't run forever, my love," Morticia replied. "I want a home again. I want our children to grow up in peace. I want to pick out cemetery plots."

Whump!

The car gave a huge lurch as it hit something heavy, then screeched to a stop at the side of the road.

Morticia, Gomez, and Thing hurried out of the car. About fifty feet back, a huge body was lying in the center of the road. It was an enormous man wearing a hospital gown and a straitjacket. He was out cold.

Gomez turned him over. The back of the straitjacket had the words State Hospital for the Criminally Insane stenciled on it.

Morticia looked up, and—how had she missed it before? The fog had parted for a moment. Looming up from the top of a hill beyond a wrought iron gate was a gothic monstrosity. A hulking, ornate wreck of a building set just far back enough from the road to feel *really* unfriendly. It had a crooked steeple and a million broken windows. Sudden lightning lit up the sky, and the house seemed to bend and warp in the flickering light.

"Oh, thank goodness," Morticia said. "A decent place to sleep for the night."

A faded sign hanging from the gate banged in the wind. State Hospital for the Criminally Insane, it read. The building had clearly been lying empty for a long time, with the apparent exception of the hulking wreck of a man they'd struck with their car.

Said wreck was now peeling himself off the pavement and lumbering toward Morticia and Gomez. His arms were held stiffly out in front of him, and he gave a cavernous howl.

"NNNNYYYAAAAAGH," the hulk roared. He was close enough to crush Morticia and Gomez in one motion.

Gomez smiled cheerfully and stuffed their bags into his hands.

"Thank you, old boy," he said. "Lead the way!"

The monster looked down at the bags, surprised. Then he shrugged and led Morticia and Gomez through the gate and toward the abandoned insane asylum.

Morticia smiled happily. How convenient that they

had found a house that already had a butler! She watched him lurch up the path. Lurch . . . what a perfect name. Lurch the butler.

Morticia took Gomez's arm, and they followed Lurch to the front door of the house. Gomez gallantly swept the Police Line: Do Not Cross tape away from the front door, and they stepped in.

Stale, cold air and absolute silence greeted them. Then a faint sound came through the blackness: the scratching of rats scampering in the walls.

Morticia's eyes adjusted to the dark. She squinted down the front hall. There was a chalk outline of a body near the staircase.

"It's creepy," Gomez said thoughtfully. "Kooky."

Morticia looked up and caught the eye of a taxidermic moose head. It winked at her.

"Mysterious," she agreed. "Spooky."

Plop! Plop! Blood dripped from the ceiling.

Gomez brushed a spider the size of a pigeon off his shoulder. "It's altogether . . . what's the word?" he murmured, looking thoughtful.

Lurch lumbered up to the pipe organ at the top of the grand staircase. Thing scurried over and hopped up onto the keyboard. Together, the two of them plunked out the few notes of a decidedly twisted little tune.

"*GETTTTTTTTT OUTTTTTTT*," a voice like a sinking ship moaned, interrupting the music. It seemed to come from every hall, from every nook and every cranny. The whole house trembled.

Morticia and Gomez jumped.

"It's hideous!" Morticia exclaimed.

"It's horrible!" Gomez agreed.

"It's *home*," they sighed in unison. Gomez dipped Morticia into a dramatic kiss in the doorway of their dream house, and Lurch took up the odd little tune again, with Thing snapping in cheerful rhythm.

CHAPTER 1

THIRTEEN YEARS LATER . . .

A thick fog still wrapped itself around the hill. Anyone passing by the wrought iron gate would be surprised to discover that a hulking house lurked beyond the blanket of mist. But nobody ever stopped to investigate . . . and nobody had even noticed that the old asylum sign had been replaced with a new sign:

The Addams Family

The sun was rising, but no light reached the house at the top of the hill. The clouds wrapped around it far too snugly. And to make matters worse—or better, if you were an Addams—a torrential downpour was falling on this particular morning.

Morticia threw open the window and smiled as a sheet of freezing rain hit her square in the face.

"What a lovely morning!" she exclaimed cheerfully. The window slammed itself shut, barely missing Morticia's fingers. She smiled slyly.

"Nice try," she murmured. The spirit of the house had been doing its best to wound, maim, or kill the Addamses since they'd moved in. Morticia found it extremely charming. She'd always wanted to live in a haunted house—you were never home alone with a poltergeist, after all.

"*GET OUUUUT.*" The hollow, echoing scream floated through the corridors of the house. Morticia rolled her eyes affectionately.

"Oh, you're always so grumpy before your morning coffee," she said. She picked up the coffee pot she'd brought upstairs from the kitchen for just this purpose and walked into the bathroom.

Plsh—Morticia carefully poured the steaming black coffee into the toilet and flushed it.

"Better?" she asked.

"*AAAAAAAAAAH,*" sighed the house. The floorboards

and rafters creaked softly as the entire building settled down and began to vibrate very gently.

Morticia patted the doorframe affectionately.

The house had been fed. Now it was time for the children. She pressed a button on a call box mounted on the wall.

"Lurch," Morticia murmured into the speaker, "it's time for breakfast."

Several stories down, in the sub-sub-basement of the former asylum, Lurch sat on his bed, reading. It had been thirteen years since the Addamses had hit him with their car on that fateful night, and he had been their loyal butler ever since. It beat wandering around an abandoned mental asylum, after all. Lurch gently placed the book next to his other books and groaned as he sat up. With a great creaking and popping of joints, the hulking zombie of a man stood up and shuffled out of the padded cell he called a bedroom, his head scraping along the mattress-covered ceiling.

Morticia's next stop was the office, to find Thing. The disembodied hand jumped when she opened the door.

"Thing!" Morticia said. "Have Ichabod wake the children."

She swept down the hallway, and Thing scuttled along ahead of her, swinging open a window and nimbly climbing out of it. Meanwhile, Morticia continued her morning rounds. She caught up with Lurch as he emerged from the kitchen with the breakfast tray. Once the meal was on the table, Morticia sent Lurch off on another task.

"It's time to begin dusting up for the party," she said. There wasn't that much time left before the big event, and Morticia wanted everything to look *perfect*. Lurch nodded and obediently headed down the hall to fetch the vacuum cleaner. He looked at the wall critically as he went—a single droplet of blood was trickling down the wallpaper. Lurch shook his head and sighed. Poltergeists. He banged the wall a couple of times with his fist, and the entire surface began oozing blood.

There, that was better.

The old, broken vacuum cleaner was stored in the closet off the pantry. When Lurch turned it on, it began spewing dust all over everything. Lurch nodded in satisfaction. He carefully pointed it at the couch, then at the candelabra, then finally at the picture frames on the wall. Soon the room was coated in a thick blanket of stale-smelling dust. It looked perfect. Lurch almost smiled, his cheeks creaking stiffly, before his face went back to its usual wooden blankness. He continued dusting.

The racket of the vacuum cleaner roared through the west wing of the house, but on the second story, in the east wing, everything was quiet and peaceful. Two children slept snug in their beds. Ten-year-old Pugsley was huddled under his covers, his head shoved under his pillow. Nearby, in her own room, his thirteen-year-old sister Wednesday slept sweetly in a bed rigged under a guillotine, her bare neck stretched out under the razor-sharp blade.

First the window to Pugsley's room slid open, then the window to Wednesday's. As the two children slept, wooden tentacles slipped into their rooms through the open windows. Smooth, grasping vines crept across the floor and hovered for a moment over the children's sleeping forms.

Then, with a mighty *SNAP*, the branches sprang into action. They twined around the kids and tore them out of their beds, pulling them out of their windows and dangling them in the air twenty feet over the ground!

"*AAAAAHHHH!*" shrieked Wednesday and Pugsley. The tree—whose branches were holding the children like rag dolls—quaked in silent laughter.

Wednesday recovered first. "All right, Ichabod," she said, rolling her eyes. "I'm awake."

The tree—Ichabod—gave her a gentle shake, as

though to say "Good morning!"

"Not for long," Pugsley commented, flinging a hatchet at his sister cheerfully. Wednesday snatched it out of the air before it hit her and twirled it in her fingers. "Real mature, Pugsley," she said scornfully. She sighed, bored. The Addams family had a proud tradition of doing their best to kill each other. They never succeeded, of course, but it was fun to try, and a healthy spirit of competition (and mortal peril) kept the days lively. But Pugsley's attempt with the hatchet had been lackluster. It took more than a badly thrown axe to really wake Wednesday up.

"How I wish something would liven up this already tedious day," she said, and yawned.

Ichabod gave a tree-ish shrug and threw Pugsley through the air back toward the house. Pugsley sailed through his open window and landed on his bed with an "Oof!"

Wednesday tilted her head. "Thanks for trying, Ichabod," she said. She patted the branch that was still holding her. The tree gently let her down, and she wandered toward the house.

But before Wednesday could make it very far, a strange noise caught her attention.

Brrring! Brrring!

It sounded like . . . a bicycle bell? And it was coming from down the hill, where the driveway gate separated the house grounds from the local road.

Wednesday wandered down through the permanent bank of fog toward the gate. She'd never heard anything other than the occasional noisy car motor, and she was curious. Who was there? Had someone stopped at the gate? Why? The fog thickened as she got closer to the gate—soon it was impossible to see farther than five feet in front of her.

Brrring! Brrring!

The bicycle bell sounded again. Someone was hidden in the fog on the other side of the gate and was ringing their bell—in a strange way, it felt like someone was saying hello.

Reaching through the dense fog, Wednesday knocked on the gate in reply.

Clang. Clang.

Wednesday held her breath and listened as closely as she could. A soft gasp sounded from the fog on the other side of the gate. Someone *was* there! Then Wednesday heard the sound of pedals turning, a bicycle chain going taut, and the low hiss of rubber bicycle wheels against the pavement—

Whoever it was was riding away.

Disappointed, Wednesday turned and headed back up through the moat of fog to the towering house on the hill, where breakfast was waiting.

Back up at the house, Pugsley was hiding in the top room of the tallest tower of the house. He had a trunk full of explosives next to him, and a telescope in his hand. He peered through the telescope, seeking, seeking—aha! There he was.

"Pugsley! Pugsley!" Below, in the garden, Gomez Addams wandered around the house grounds looking for his son. "Pugsley!"

Up in the tower, Pugsley smiled. "Let the games begin," he murmured.

"Pugsley!" Gomez called as he rounded the side of the house and headed toward the hedge. "It's time for sword practice!"

Flooom!

Behind Gomez, a great plume of smoke and fire emerged from the house as a rocket launched from the tower. Pugsley, riding the rocket like a bronco, gave a great "Yee-haw!" as it tore into the sky. The rocket shot straight up, then slowed and reached the top of its trajectory. For one breathless moment, it hung perfectly still in the air. Pugsley held on tight as the rocket began to fall. Faster, faster, it sped down to earth, aimed straight at Gomez.

"Death to the oppressor!" Pugsley screeched as the missile neared his father.

At the last moment, Gomez dodged backward. Pugsley yanked the rocket's nose up so it wouldn't crash into the ground and rode it into the sky for another dive. His father stumbled, recovering from his first dodge, as Pugsley drove the rocket at him again. Gomez ducked again—another near miss. He sprang back to his feet and shook his head impatiently.

"All right, son, that's enough," Gomez said sternly.

But Pugsley couldn't hear him. The rocket was sailing up, up, up, spiraling out of control as it tore into the clouds. Gomez watched with some curiosity as the rocket disappeared into the clouds, and then—

Boom!

A distant explosion flashed high in the sky as the rocket finally exploded. Gomez squinted into the sunlight, scanning the sky for his son.

"Yeaaaaa*AAAAAGH*!" Pugsley appeared, his scream getting louder and louder as he fell closer and closer to earth. When he was only about a hundred feet above the ground, Pugsley yanked the cord on his emergency parachute vest, and a large silk parachute popped open above him. He dangled from the parachute, gliding gently and slowly downward.

Not wasting a moment, Pugsley pulled out his slingshot and a handful of small explosive mines and began hurling the mines at his father. *Blam! Blam! Blam!* The mines landed around Gomez as he danced and dodged and, finally, fled.

"Don't make me come up there!" Gomez shouted up at Pugsley, who sailed through the sky hanging from his parachute, shooting down more mines at his father.

"This is your last warning!" Gomez called, still running.

Pugsley rummaged in his pocket. Only one mine left. He fitted it into the strap of his slingshot and pulled it back, taking aim carefully. As Pugsley released the mine, Gomez pulled a baseball bat out of nowhere and turned to face the incoming explosive. He waggled the bat, took a batting stance, and waited.

Bam! Gomez hit the mine straight back at Pugsley, and it detonated in the parachute, sending Pugsley spinning down into the greenhouse, where he landed with a *crash*.

Gomez gave him a hand up.

"Morning," he said.

"Morning," Pugsley replied cheerfully.

Gomez took his son by the shoulders and stared seriously into his eyes. "Pugsley," he said. "We're supposed to be working on your swordplay every morning before breakfast. Your Sabre Mazurka is in two weeks, and you've barely practiced at all!"

Pugsley pouted and shrugged. "So I missed one practice. What's the big deal?"

Gomez's eyes went wide. "The *big deal*?!" he cried. "Why, the Sabre Mazurka is the most important day in the life of a young Addams man! It's what *makes* you an Addams! It's the day your *entire family* gathers around you and *judges your worth as a human being*."

"It's basically Thanksgiving," Wednesday offered as she trooped by them on her way into the house.

"There!" Gomez agreed. "Thanksgiving! Whatever that is."

Pugsley squirmed. "But swords are so old-fashioned," he whined. "I'm more of a demolitions man."

Gomez frowned sternly. "Explosives have no place in a Mazurka," he said. "Hand them over."

Pugsley sighed and handed his father a stick of TNT.

"All of it," Gomez prompted, and Pugsley rummaged

through his clothes and produced another stick of TNT, a handful of M-80s, several roman candles, some bang-snaps, a holy hand grenade, and a small pile of other miscellaneous explosives.

"Is that all of it?" Gomez asked sternly.

Pugsley nodded. "I swear on my honor as an Addams," he said.

Gomez nodded his head, satisfied. He knelt down and took Pugsley by the shoulders. "Son," he said gently, "our family hasn't been all together in thirteen years. Not since your mother and I got married. They're all coming from all over the world to see *you* on your special day."

Pugsley stared up at his father, his eyes wide.

"I just want it to go perfectly," Gomez said.

"Okay, Pop," Pugsley said softly. "I'll practice."

"That's my boy," Gomez replied, and gave him a hearty pat on the back. It knocked a stick of TNT out of Pugsley's pocket.

"Oops," Pugsley said insincerely.

CHAPTER 2

Morticia sat down at the breakfast table with a happy sigh. Family breakfast—her favorite time of day. Gomez snapped open a hundred-year-old newspaper, releasing a cloud of moths, and began to read. Wednesday and Pugsley kicked each other under the table. And Lurch slumped in and swept the silver cover off the breakfast platter with a flourish.

A fetid, horrible smell emerged from the platter.

"Putrid," Morticia said approvingly. Lurch smiled and nodded his thanks.

"Horrifying," Gomez agreed. Morticia smiled at him.

Truly, they were so lucky to have a cook as talented as Lurch tending to their meals. Today's breakfast smelled like it had spent a few weeks in an overheated funeral home.

As they ate, Morticia began sorting through the mail that had arrived over the past week.

"Gomez," she said, "everyone we've invited to Pugsley's Mazurka has threatened to come."

Gomez beamed. "Wonderful!" he said. "All the Addamses and Frumps under one roof again!" He ducked as Pugsley flung a hatchet at his head. It hit the back of Gomez's chair with a *twang*.

"Yes," Morticia replied, "but where will everyone sleep?"

Gomez grinned. "We'll have Lurch fix up the mausoleum," he suggested. "It'll be like sleep-away camp!"

Morticia plucked a beeping time bomb out of the pile of envelopes and tossed it casually over her shoulder. It flew out the open window and detonated outside with an earth-shaking *BANG*.

Grass and dirt flew everywhere, a few rocks pelted into the sky, and a man's body flew through the window—glass exploding into the breakfast nook—and landed on the ground in a heap.

Whump.

The man sprang to his feet and brushed glass out of his clothing. "It's okay!" he said. "I'm okay; the plate glass window broke my fall."

"Uncle Fester!" Pugsley cried, and leapt out of his chair to greet his uncle.

"Brother!" Gomez said, standing and hugging Fester. "I'm thrilled you're here!"

"I'm not late, am I?" Fester asked.

"Actually," Morticia said a little tartly, "we weren't expecting you for another two weeks." She shot a sharp look at Gomez, who winced.

"I apologize, darling," he said. "I asked Fester to come early to help Pugsley with his Mazurka practice."

Morticia sighed impatiently. Men. They never thought of the ways they inconvenienced their wives. They knew nothing about the rules of hospitality.

"If I'd known you were coming," she said apologetically to Fester, "I would have prepared the dungeon."

"Please," Fester said hurriedly, "don't worry about that. I'll just sleep in the attic. You won't even know I'm here. I mean, you'll have *no idea*." He grinned. "I've practiced that move in a lot of people's homes. Most of them never caught on—not even after *years*."

Fester turned to greet the Addams children. "I can't believe it!" he said. "The last time I saw you, you were *this tall*." He measured off about a foot with his hands.

"That's because you buried us up to our necks," Pugsley reminded him.

"Ooh, riiiiight," Fester said, staring off into space sentimentally. "And then those spiders came and laid eggs in your mouths!"

Wednesday nodded.

"Isn't family special?" Fester said.

"Uncle," Wednesday said thoughtfully, "can you tell us what's beyond the gate?"

Lurch, who was on his way out of the room with the breakfast tray, stopped in his tracks and dropped it. Morticia set her fork down on her plate with a sharp *clang*. She turned to Wednesday.

"Why would you ask that, dear?" Morticia asked in a voice that was trying—and failing—to sound casual.

Wednesday shrugged. "I heard a strange noise in the fog earlier," she said. "I want to investigate."

Morticia shook her head sharply. "There's nothing out there but boring marshland," she said.

Wednesday knew she was pushing it. But she kept

going. "But there must be *something*," she said. "We never go *anywhere*. Who knows what untold horrors we're missing out on!"

Morticia laid a hand on her daughter's hand. "We have all the horror we need right here, my love," she said.

Wednesday scowled. "Uncle Fester gets to go wherever *he* wants," she said rebelliously.

"Now, now," Fester broke in. "That's not quite true. There are some legal restrictions. For example, I can't go to a mall. Or a school. Or a public park. Or—"

Morticia broke in. "When you're older, Wednesday," she said firmly, "you can travel to your heart's content. But for now, it's safer for you here."

Wednesday knew when she was beat.

"Socrates," she said, calling over her pet octopus, "come."

With the octopus slinking along behind her, Wednesday slouched out of the dining room and went back up to her room.

MEANWHILE . . .

What Morticia referred to as "boring marshland" was actually a suburban neighborhood called Eastfield Estates, not far from the mist-shrouded hill the Addamses' house stood on. Eastfield Estates was a peaceful, safe, and adorable neighborhood. So, to be fair, Morticia's description of it as a "boring marshland" was fairly accurate . . . from the point of view of an Addams.

At that very moment, a reality television show was being shot right there in that boring marshland, in an *incredibly* boring house.

Design Intervention.

The host, Margaux Needler, patted her blow-dried hair into place, checked her cardigan sweater for lint, straightened her tool belt, turned to the camera, and pasted a big, fake smile onto her face

"I'm here to help," she announced, her smile never wavering. "I take your uninspired living space and turn it into the perfect palace of your dreams. No matter how outdated your design sense, I can help you."

She strode through the house, and the camera crew followed her. Her frozen smile grew bigger with each step she took.

"My only flaw?" She paused, and amped up her smile even further. "Sometimes I care *too* much."

Margaux left the house and began walking through the adorable little town. As she talked, the cameras passed parks, sweet little pastel houses, neatly trimmed lawns, and a wide variety of songbirds singing in the perfectly pruned trees.

"I'm Margaux Needler," she said, "and I'm about to stage a Design Intervention." She winked at the camera. "You're welcome in advance."

Margaux—and the cameras—walked through a cute little "downtown" area, with a yoga-clothing shop, an old-fashioned soda fountain, and seven different storefront banks. "Today," she continued, "we're putting the finishing touches on our biggest project yet. Eastfield Estates." She waved her arm, gesturing to the entire neighborhood. "We didn't just make over a house—we made over a *whole town*! Eastfield is here to show what a great neighborhood looks like. It's as flawless as my hair! And who wouldn't like to live in my hair?"

The cameramen looked at each other, wincing. Sometimes Margaux went a little too far.

She led the cameras into the town square.

"In just two weeks, on our live season finale," she continued, "*you* will be able to buy your very own piece of Eastfield. That's right—in a *Design Intervention* first, we are putting a *whole neighborhood* up for sale. This will be your chance to purchase the house of your dreams . . . in the town of your dreams."

Margaux slowed to a stop in front of a group of towns-folk who just "happened" to have gathered at the town square. They all waved hello to the cameras.

"Sound good?" Margaux said to the cameras. "I thought so. Welcome to Eastfield—*neighbor.*"

The crowd gave a big cheer. Confetti flew through the air, and hundreds of balloons flew into the sky.

"Aaaaaand . . . we're out!" Glenn, the producer, yelled.

Margaux let the smile drop off her face. It was immediately replaced with a sour scowl.

Glenn hurried up to her as the crew began putting the cameras and equipment away. "Love it," he said, "Love it, love it. Perfect. Margaux, did that feel good to you?"

Margaux narrowed her eyes. "*Must* we with the balloons and confetti, Glenn?" she asked. "It's a bit much."

"They're great!" he protested. "*You're* great. It's all great!"

Margaux glared at him. "They *better* be great, because if we don't sell all these houses, you and I are *finished.*"

Glenn gulped nervously. They'd invested a *lot* of money in redoing the houses in Eastfield Estates, it was true. If people didn't buy those houses right away, it would be very, very bad. But they had done everything right! The houses all had glossy tile in the bathrooms and granite countertops in the kitchens. They all had recessed lighting in the living rooms and cheerful throw blankets on the couches. The yards were green and smooth, and they'd even drained the nearby marsh to make room for a golf course. How could it fail?

Margaux's phone rang, and she eagerly answered it, her big fake smile lighting up her face.

"You're welcome in advance!" she said, nodding and grinning and staring vacantly into space as the other person talked.

At that moment, a girl on a bike rode up. *Brrring! Brrring!* She rang the bike's bell excitedly and waved to get Margaux's attention. Margaux ignored her.

"Mom!" the girl said. "Mom! You're never going to believe this! I rode up the back road, up that hill? And I found this dirt road, and there was all this fog, and there was this *gate*, and I think there's some kind of weird old mansion up there!"

Margaux finished her call and hung up the phone. She looked up.

"Oh," she said. "Hi, Parker. Did you say something?"

Parker bounced on her bike seat. "I *said*, I found a creepy mansion up on the hill! Really close by!"

Margaux smiled a fake smile. "I'm so glad you're exploring, Parker. I love it that you're getting into real estate like your mama! But right now I don't have time to talk. Margaux needs to *help* people."

She started to walk away. Parker hopped off her bike and grabbed at her mom's sleeve.

"*I* need help," she said. "Aren't *I* 'people'?"

"No," Margaux said impatiently, yanking her hand away. "I mean *actual* people. People who watch *television*."

Parker watched her mom go, then stormed off, kicking a red balloon out of her path.

CHAPTER 3

MEANWHILE,
UP ON THAT FOGGY HILL . . .

Pugsley had his bow-and-arrow set out and was aiming an arrow straight at Lurch, who stood with his back to a tree.

Pugsley considered just letting the arrow go and seeing what would happen, but then he reluctantly shifted his aim about a foot to the left, to the target Lurch was holding for him.

"Left a bit . . ." Pugsley said. Lurch adjusted the target. "Now down a bit . . . perfect!"

"MRGH," Lurch groaned encouragingly.

"And three . . . two . . . one . . ." Pugsley murmured,

getting ready to shoot the arrow at the target.

BWWAAAAHHHMMM!!!

Wednesday had blasted an air horn right into his ear. Pugsley jumped a mile and fired the arrow into the air. It vanished into the foggy sky, and the children heard a *thunk* and a surprised yelp as it hit Fester, who had been taking a nap.

Pugsley rounded on Wednesday. "You made me miss!" he said furiously. "Do you know how long it took for me to set this up? It took Lurch *twenty minutes* to make it to this tree from the front porch. You know how slowly he moves!"

Wednesday rolled her eyes. "Look, Pugsley," she said impatiently. "Your Mazurka is coming up, and you are *not ready*. Even if I *am* the only person who can see it. So pay attention, kid, and do exactly what I say, and you might actually get through this."

Pugsley stared at his sister. "Wait," he said incredulously. "You're going to *help* me? Why?"

Wednesday's mouth pursed like she was tasting something bad. "Because you're my *brother*," she spat out, "and I *love you*."

"You need help," Pugsley said nervously.

"You need it worse," Wednesday retorted. "Now, you see that hole over there? Go stand by it."

Pugsley walked over to the freshly dug hole in the yard. It was about the size of a grave.

"This one?" he asked.

"That one," Wednesday said. She had an unpleasant smile on her face.

"I don't get it—" Pugsley started, before he got distracted by a mysterious red sphere that floated by his head. "Hey," he said, "what's—"

But he was cut off by Wednesday smashing a shovel across the back of his head and knocking him out cold.

Clang.

Wednesday emptied the last shovelful of dirt onto the refilled grave and patted the mound of soil happily. "Sleep tight," she murmured.

Pugsley had taken the bait—hook, line, and sinker. He'd really believed that she wanted to help him with his Mazurka! What a sap.

Wednesday turned away from the grave and examined her new prize. She'd grabbed it as soon as she'd knocked out Pugsley, and tied it to a bush so she could investigate it later. It was about the size and shape of a human head, but it was round and smooth and red and . . . it floated. Wednesday had never seen anything like it. She loved it.

She headed inside.

"Good news, everybody," she announced to her parents. "Pugsley's gone."

Morticia sighed. "Wednesday, I know that tone of voice," she said. "Dig your brother up at once."

Wednesday scowled. Was she that transparent? She needed to try out some new murder weapons on Pugsley, obviously. And her parents needed to stop interfering.

"You're weakening the gene pool," she said sulkily. Then her mother spotted the red . . . *thing* she was holding.

"What do you have there?" Morticia asked Wednesday. Wednesday looked up at it. It was kind of like a ball, but lighter, and more delicate. She still had no idea what it was.

"I'm not sure," Wednesday said. "I like it, though. It's so . . ." She struggled for the right word. "What's the opposite of *gloomy*?"

Morticia took the ball. "It's a *balloon*," she said, in the tone of voice most people use to identify a dead rat. "How strange that it's here all by itself. There's usually a murderous clown attached to the other end of these."

Then Morticia gasped in horror. Wednesday watched, alarmed, as her mother reached a shaking hand toward her.

"Wednesday," she whispered, her face even more ashen than usual, "don't move."

She plucked something from Wednesday's shoulder. It was a small fragment of brightly colored pink paper.

"What in the name of all that is unholy is *that*?" asked Gomez. He took the bit of paper from Morticia and gingerly put his tongue out to taste it.

"It tastes like cotton candy," Gomez said, looking horrified.

"What on earth is going *on*?" Morticia said. She and Gomez hurried outside to investigate, and Wednesday trailed after them, still clutching her . . . what had her mother called it?

Oh, yes. Her *balloon*.

Outside, the wind was still sweeping up the hill, and now it was carrying hundreds—thousands—millions?—of those little scraps of paper.

Fester stared up at the sky.

"Confetti," he said in horror. "I saw something like this in the jungles of Florida once. There's a torture camp there called—"

"Gah!" Pugsley gasped as he erupted from the grave Wednesday had buried him in. He shook dirt out of his hair and looked up at the shower of . . . *confetti*.

"What is that?" he asked, squinting in confusion. "Where is it coming from?"

Wednesday pointed silently down the driveway. The gate, usually shrouded in fog, was clearly visible.

The fog was gone.

"Wait," Gomez said, confused. "The fog is lifting!"

"That would only happen if—" Morticia started.

"If someone drained the marsh!" Gomez finished. "But who would do that? And why?"

They squinted down the hill. As the fog continued to thin, a horrifying vision was revealed.

An adorable suburban town.

"A town," Morticia said. "A . . . *normal* town. This is not good."

Gomez squared his shoulders. He was clearly determined to make the best of this disastrous development. "We must go down there and introduce ourselves at once!" he said bravely.

Wednesday stared down at the newly revealed town, then up at her parents. "This day is becoming most wonderfully disruptive," she said happily.

Down in Eastfield Estates, producer Glenn caught up to Margaux Needler in front of one of the new houses she had built in Eastfield. "I've just gotten confirmation that they've finished draining the swamp," he told her.

Margaux nodded. "Just in time!" she said. "That filthy swamp stank up my whole town." She smirked. "And now we can put in a golf course."

"Exactly!" Glenn said, smiling happily.

Margaux pulled Glenn into the house. "I can't wait to reveal these new houses on the show," she said. "People are going to lose their minds when they see the picture window in this living room."

She went and posed in front of the curtained window. "When we shoot the next scene," she told Glenn, "we'll do a sequence with me standing in front of this window, like this."

She reached out and took the curtain in one hand. "And then I'll do a big dramatic reveal where I pull the curtain open and they can see the incredible view!"

With a flourish, Margaux pulled the curtain open. "Like this!" she said, and grinned her big television grin.

But Glenn did not grin back. He just stared out the window. Horror dawned on his face.

"What," Margaux snapped. "What's the matter? Do I have something in my teeth?"

Then she turned, and horror swept over her face as well.

Perfectly framed in the brand-new picture window was

a hulking gothic mansion slumped on the top of a dark, rocky hill.

Lightning streaked across the sky, reflecting off the broken windows of the hideous home. The hideous home now revealed to be in eyesight from every single house for sale in Eastfield Estates.

Margaux shrieked.

CHAPTER 4

The Addamses didn't leave their house very often. Or, to tell the truth, ever.

So it took a little while to get everything organized for their trip down to Eastfield Estates. Wednesday wanted to bring her pet octopus, Socrates. But then Kitty, the family's semi-pet lion ("semi" because the word "pet" suggests "tame," which Kitty . . . wasn't), wanted to come. And then, because Socrates *and* Kitty were both going, Ichabod the tree wanted to come too.

It took some doing to explain to Ichabod that trees can't ride in cars. Eventually, Wednesday agreed to leave

Socrates back home to keep Ichabod company, and the Addamses—Morticia, Gomez, Fester, Wednesday, Pugsley, and Kitty—all piled into the car, with Lurch at the wheel.

Two minutes later, they were pulling up to a pedestrian mall at the heart of Eastfield Estates. Kitty bounded out of the car.

"Play nice!" Gomez called after him as citizens screamed and scrambled to get away from him.

The Addamses all piled out of the car and stood in the painfully bright sunlight, blinking and looking around the charming little town. Fester wandered off. Gomez didn't bother following him—there weren't that many places Fester could legally go, anyway.

"What kind of topsy-turvy place is this?" Gomez said. "There isn't even a gallows in the town square."

Morticia looked around at all the new construction. Half of the buildings had been built in the last few years, and the older ones were all very nicely kept up. She sniffed critically. "It'll be years before rust and decay set in," she said. "Who would want to live here?"

But Wednesday didn't feel the same way at all. She saw the clean streets, the white pavement sidewalks, the emerald-green lawns, and the cheerful flower beds, and something inside of her perked up. It was the strangest sensation—Wednesday had never in her entire life experienced anything close to perkiness.

"It's all so . . . *different*," she breathed.

Pugsley spotted a bowl of water with a dog-paw pattern printed on it, set out on the sidewalk in front of a shop. "At least they're generous to traveling strangers," he said, getting down on all fours to lap some of the water up. A man walking by stopped and stared at Pugsley.

"Whose child is this?" he asked, looking around.

Morticia blushed scarlet and hurried over. "Pugsley! Manners!" she cried, pulling him up. "Don't drink it all. This gentleman wants some too."

Pugsley wiped his mouth on his sleeve. "Sorry," he said. He smiled at the man. "It's all yours," he added, pointing at the remaining water in the bowl on the ground.

The man stared at him, then at Morticia, and then turned and ran.

"What a nervous fellow," Morticia murmured.

"Come on, Tish!" Gomez said cheerfully. "Let's explore the neighborhood!"

Morticia looked around skeptically. "Must we?" she asked.

Gomez shrugged. "You don't have to, darling," he said. "But I'd like to meet our new neighbors." He looked around, wondering where to start. "Ah!" he said, pointing at a coffee shop. "I'm going to pop in here for a minute, and I'll meet you all in the town square. Sound good?"

"Very well, dear," Morticia said nervously, drawing Wednesday and Pugsley close to her. She looked around the bright, cheerful little town with dark suspicion.

"Stay close, children," she told them. "Don't make any sudden movements."

Gomez swanned into the local café and bowed to the people inside. They all stopped talking and stared at him.

"Good day!" he said loudly. "Don't let me interrupt your, ah, *cup of Joe*, or whoever you've trapped in there." He pointed to an urn of coffee. "Poor fellow," he added.

He turned to the barista. "Coffeemaster!" he exclaimed. "Sell me something dark and bitter."

The barista stared at him blankly. "Uh," she said. Then she snapped back into customer service mode. "We have a single-source, renewably green Madagascar peaberry with notes of oak, cherry, and yoga."

Gomez thought about it. "Sounds awful," he said encouragingly. "But you know, I think I'm looking for something stronger."

One of the other baristas was emptying a vat of used

coffee grounds into the trash, and Gomez hurried over to him. "Ah!" Gomez said. "That looks delicious. Let me try that."

Margaux and Glenn drove through Eastfield in an adorable golf cart. Margaux gripped the wheel, her knuckles white. She was grinding her teeth with rage. Glenn scrolled desperately through his phone, reading through an archive of public records.

"Ah!" he said finally. "Here it is. That house is owned by a Gomez and Morticia Addams."

Margaux bared her teeth. Now she knew the names of her enemies. "Why am I only hearing about this now?" she demanded. "Every neighbor in the neighborhood counts. If this neighborhood is not *perfection*, these home values will *plummet*, and we will lose a *lot of money*, Glenn."

Glenn continued reading the record on his phone. "I'm not sure why we didn't know about them before," he said. "The rest of this property record just says 'AAAAAAAAAAAAAAH!'."

Margaux squinted. "I know exactly what needs to be done here," she said.

* * *

48

Gomez strolled along the main street of Eastfield Estates, eating coffee grounds with a spoon. His face lit up when he spotted Morticia standing exactly in the center of the town square, her bony arms wrapped protectively around Wednesday and Pugsley. She looked like a trapped feral cat ready to scratch. Gomez smiled fondly. What a lovely woman she was.

"Morticia!" he cried as he strode toward her. "You really must try these coffee grounds. They're fantastic!"

Before Morticia could reply, a shrill chorus of voices intruded on the quiet afternoon.

"Hooray, join the party! This is where we all belong!"

Gomez's coffee grounds dropped from his suddenly nerveless fingers. He stared around in shock. He'd never heard such an awful noise in his life.

"Everybody come together and sing our song, sing our song!" the little piping voices continued. Gomez fought the urge to cover his ears with his hands.

Morticia looked as disturbed as he felt. "What am I *hearing*?" she said, appalled.

Gomez gathered his family together, and they looked around cautiously. "I think the path is clear to the car," Gomez said. "Let's run for it."

But when they rounded the corner, they found the source of the noise: a children's choir.

The children of Eastfield Estates were wearing bright polo shirts, matching hats, and khaki shorts. They were performing in front of a gazebo in a nicely manicured little park. A banner hanging behind them read CHIPPER AND CHEER FUNDRAISER. Some of the townspeople had gathered to listen to the mind-bending din.

"That is absolutely horrible," Gomez said. His initial fear had faded, and now he was just sort of in awe of how awful the sound was. Fester wandered over, both hands firmly over his ears.

"What an upsetting noise!" he bellowed at Gomez. Gomez could only nod. What on earth did these children think they were *doing*?

"*It's easy to be happy when you have no choice!*" the children went on.

Realization dawned slowly. Gomez knew exactly what was happening.

"Hold on!" Gomez said, turning to Morticia. "Unless I miss my guess here, I believe this is supposed to be *music*."

"What?" Morticia said.

"Yes!" Gomez continued. Suddenly it all made sense. "They're greeting us with one of their traditional songs!"

Fester beamed. "Well, then," he said, "*we* oughta do the same!"

Morticia smiled. "What a wonderful idea, Fester," she said.

Fester walked up to the choir. They stopped singing, confused, and watched as he reached into his coat.

He pulled out two bats and used their squeaky shrieks as an accompaniment for his cacophonous singing.

The chorus screamed and ran.

Fester watched them go, forlorn. Tears sprang into his eyes. He turned to Gomez. "What did I do?" he asked woefully.

Morticia frowned. "How rude," she said. "Screaming and running away after Fester's lovely offering. Perhaps we should return home."

She began hurrying toward the car, but Gomez caught her by the arm. "Morticia," he murmured. "This is not the old country, dearest. True, these people are a little *different* from us, but deep down we're all the same."

A local man screamed as he ran across the park lawn, pursued by a roaring Kitty.

Gomez went on: "There seem to be many empty houses in this town. And the local populace appears to be largely peaceful. This could be a wonderful place for our extended family to stay for the Mazurka . . ." He raised his eyebrows at Morticia. She nodded reluctantly. It wasn't a bad idea. "We have to give them a chance," Gomez coaxed. "Get to know them. Win them over."

Morticia snorted. "Win them over," she repeated. That had worked *so well* in the old country . . .

Screeee! A golf cart slammed to a stop on the sidewalk by the park, and an aggressively blow-dried woman leapt out, followed by an apologetic-looking man with a headset and a name tag that said Glenn on it.

"Well, good morning, neighbor!" the woman chirped as she strode toward the Addamses. "I'm Margaux Needler."

Gomez stepped forward and offered his hand. "Gomez Addams," he said, "at your service." He gestured to Morticia, who was glaring at Margaux. "My wife, Morticia."

Morticia gave Margaux a look that could have frozen a lake of lava. "Charmed," she said.

Gomez ignored her tone. "And our children, Wednesday and Pugsley," he said, gesturing to the kids. "And my brother, Fester."

Fester stepped forward. "Hey, neighbor!" he said to Margaux, who had instinctively shrunk back. He was still clutching the two bats. "You know we can see right into your windows?"

Margaux blanched, but she recovered quickly. It wasn't a coincidence that she was one of the top reality television stars in the world. She knew how to lie.

"Nice to meet you," she said cheerfully. "As your neighbor, I'd like to offer you the opportunity of a lifetime. How would you like a free home makeover from a world-renowned interior designer?"

Gomez Addams, Morticia Addams, Fester Addams, Wednesday Addams, Pugsley Addams, and an adult lion with no leash all stared at Margaux blankly.

There was a long, awkward silence. Then Gomez said, tentatively, "I suppose it would depend on the designer?"

Margaux huffed indignantly. Had these people never been in the same *room* as a television? How was it possible that they didn't know who she was?

"Me!" she said impatiently, and then hastily slapped a big grin over her impatient scowl. "I'm talking about *me*. It will be a challenge," she added, "but I can beautify that old house of yours so fast it'll make your head spin."

Fester brightened up at that. "I don't want to brag," he said, "but mine already does that. Look!"

He turned his head, and then kept turning it and turning it. Margaux watched in terrified fascination as his head turned completely around until he was facing her again.

He smiled. She hastily looked away.

"I should like to see what this plastic woman has to offer," the little girl—Wednesday, Margaux reminded herself—said thoughtfully. She seemed to be about the same age as Margaux's daughter, Parker. Margaux forced herself to smile at the child. "Well, aren't you adorable," she said. "I love your dress. Where did you get it?"

Wednesday smiled stiffly. "It's just something I dug up," she said. Margaux looked more closely and noticed traces of soil still clinging to the hem. She winced and moved a few steps farther away from the little girl.

"Yes, well," she said nervously. Who *were* these people? They got weirder with every minute.

Margaux turned to the mother—Morticia. "When is a good time to stop by?" she asked.

Morticia stiffened. "Actually, Ms. Needler," she started. She was clearly about to refuse the offer, but before she could get the words out, her husband elbowed her gently. "Darling," he muttered softly.

Morticia paused. She smiled at Margaux through gritted teeth. "Stop by any time you'd like," she said stiffly.

Margaux grinned like a shark. "Then it's settled!" she said. "I'll see you at your house first thing tomorrow!"

There. That was that. And now she could flee.

Margaux jumped back into the golf cart and sped off. She didn't bother to wait for Glenn. He could fend for himself.

The Addamses watched the golf cart speed off with Glenn running along behind it.

"That woman seems deranged," Wednesday said thoughtfully. "Her face reminds me of a death mask."

Fester nodded. "I must ask her how she does it!" he said.

CHAPTER 5

Gomez had a solemn expression on his face as he opened the antique case. He lifted the lid carefully. Inside lay a sword—an ornate ceremonial sabre. The light caught the blade and glinted across the ballroom, landing on Pugsley's face as he looked on.

Gomez looked at his only son. "Pugsley," he said, "this is the Addams family sabre. Three hundred years' worth of Addamses have danced the Mazurka with this blade."

Pugsley snatched at the sword, but Gomez slapped his hand away.

"Ah-ah," he said warningly. "Only when you've shown me you're ready."

Fester, walking into the ballroom, chimed in. "Your father was the greatest swordsman in Addams history."

Pugsley's eyes widened. Fester went on: "His Mazurka was the stuff of legends."

"But," Gomez added, "everything *you'll* need to learn is in the Mazurka handbook."

Uncle Fester opened a huge book. He looked at it thoughtfully. "Few people know that the Sabre Mazurka began as a fighting technique that helped the Addamses prevail against enemies who threatened our very existence."

Pugsley looked up at him, eyes wide.

Fester turned the pages, seeking something specific. "Aha," he said when he found it. "The steps of the dance."

He showed Pugsley the diagrams of the Sabre Mazurka steps in the book. Lurch began playing the Mazurka theme on the organ as Fester and Gomez walked Pugsley through the steps one by one.

"We start with the Toe–Heel Slash," Fester said. Gomez demonstrated, sweeping his leg out balletically.

"Then the Deadly Possum." Gomez hunkered down, drawing his arms around his head.

"Then—oh! My favorite!" Fester continued. "The Spadroon Twist!" Gomez spun around.

Fester pointed at the final diagram. "And finally," he said, "the Slash and Duck. This lets you attack and defend at the same time!" Gomez did the Slash and Duck. It was pretty spectacular, Pugsley had to admit.

Gomez straightened up, the dance over. He stared keenly at Pugsley. "You will be judged," he said, "on your bravery. Your skill. Your passion!"

Pugsley gulped nervously.

"And, oh yes," Gomez added, "I forgot to mention, while you're doing this, all the Addamses will be trying to stab you."

Pugsley broke out into a sweat. He slammed the book shut.

Gomez grinned. "It's your turn now, boy," he said. "Fester, give him the goo-goo-ga-ga baby training sword."

Fester handed Pugsley a beat-up wooden training sword. Pugsley waved it in the air experimentally. It felt totally alien in his hand.

"Pop?" he said nervously. "Has anyone ever *failed* the Mazurka?"

Gomez tilted his head thoughtfully. "Once," he said. "Your third cousin Xander."

"I've never heard of him," Pugsley said.

Gomez grinned "Exactly," he replied. "Music!"

Lurch began playing the Mazurka again.

Pugsley gripped the sword. *Toe–Heel Slash*, he thought. *How does that one go again?*

But before he could take his first step, the doorbell rang. Lurch stopped playing abruptly and stood up to answer the door. Gomez and Fester followed him.

Pugsley breathed a deep sigh of relief.

Parker Needler didn't have a lot in common with her mom. She wasn't interested in interior design, she didn't like yoga, and she loved K-pop. Basically, she and her mom were from different planets. But if there was one thing they both loved, it was being on camera. In Margaux Needler's case, being on camera meant having a team of professional union guys with a hundred thousand dollars' worth of equipment following her up the steps to the spookiest mansion Parker had ever seen.

In Parker Needler's case, it meant livestreaming the whole thing to her internet video account from her smartphone.

"Okay, guys," Parker said, peering into her phone's camera. "I'm going up to this creepy old house. If you don't hear from me in thirty minutes, send backup."

Margaux marched up the steps to the front door. "Oh, I've never seen people more in need of Margaux's help!" she said. "I'm gonna get promoted to saint after they see the charity I do for these poor people. I'm like Mother Teresa in yoga pants!"

She rang the doorbell.

There was a long pause. The camera crew all trained their cameras on the front door of the Addamses' house. Then the door very slowly creaked open, and the largest, strangest man opened it. He looked like a cross between a butler and Frankenstein's monster.

"You raaaaaang?" he moaned.

"Yeah, no," the lead cameraman said. He ripped his headset off and dropped his camera. "Life is too short. See ya." He fled down the steps but then stopped short: an adult lion was sitting square in the middle of the walk.

The cameraman stared at the lion, who growled softly. Very slowly, the cameraman bent down, retrieved his headset and his camera, and backed up the steps.

Parker caught all of it on her phone. "This is crazy, you guys," she murmured into her livestream as she filmed the entire team, including Margaux, being herded into the house by—

STRANGE LOVE

In search of a new place to call home, newlyweds Morticia and Gomez Addams choose the great state of New Jersey. When they arrive to find a mental institution escapee and an abandoned mansion, they can't believe their luck.

"It's hideous!" "It's horrible!" "It's home!"

The Addams Family
has grown to include
Wednesday and Pugsley.

It's a full house when Uncle Fester comes to visit. He is here to help Pugsley practice for the Sabre Mazurka, the traditional Addams coming-of-age ceremony.

In a town called Eastfield Estates, Margaux Needler is filming her TV show. With the help of her producer, Glenn, and with less help from her daughter, Parker, Margaux teaches the people of Eastfield how to make their homes acceptable to her very high standards.

"You're welcome in advance."

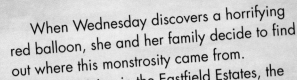

When Wednesday discovers a horrifying red balloon, she and her family decide to find out where this monstrosity came from.

After arriving in the Eastfield Estates, the Addams Family finds that everything in this strange town is extremely troubling. Everyone seems to be . . . happy.

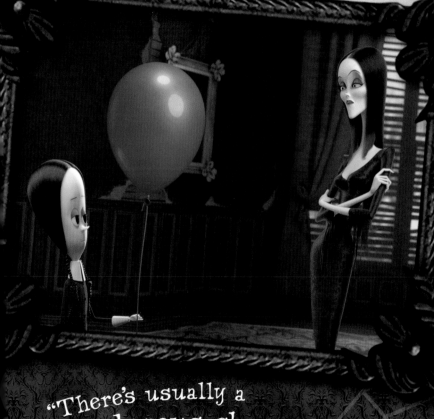

"There's usually a murderous clown attached to the other end of these."

While Gomez, Fester, and Pugsley continue to practice for the all-important Mazurka, Wednesday develops a strange fascination with this new town and her new friend, Parker.

As Wednesday spends more time with Parker, she beings to adopt some questionable fashion choices.

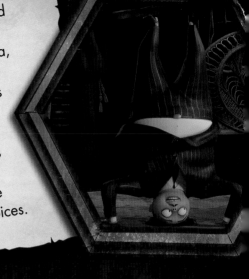

"She claims it brings out my smile."

"Wednesday, you don't have a smile."

The night before Pugsley's big Mazurka,
Wednesday decides to run away. She tells Pugsley
that she feels like the only way to be accepted in
the Addams Family is to be exactly like them.

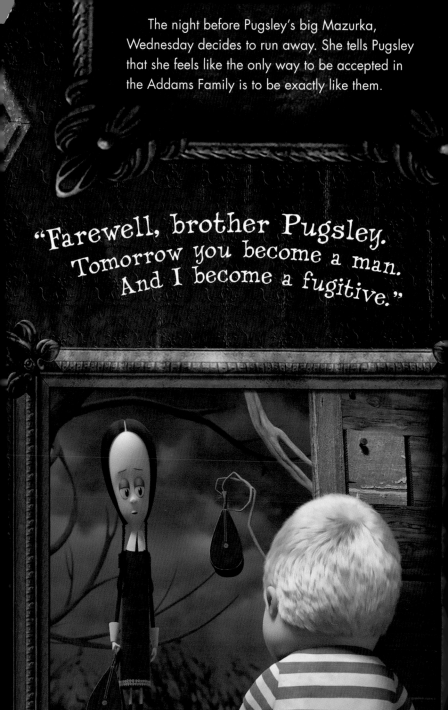

"Farewell, brother Pugsley.
Tomorrow you become a man.
And I become a fugitive."

After a secret lair is revealed and an angry mob is welcomed, the townspeople and the Addamses first set aside their differences and then learn to embrace them.

"Finally back to normal."

"Kitty!" a cheerful voice rang out. Parker turned around and saw Gomez Addams enter the hall.

"Greetings, Ms. Needler!" he continued. Parker watched from the porch as he swept up to her mother and shook her hand heartily. Then the monster butler slammed the front door shut, and Parker was alone on the porch.

She shrugged and went off to explore the grounds.

Inside the house, Morticia and Gomez were greeting their visitors.

Margaux grinned widely and insincerely. "Good morning!" she said. "I do hope this isn't a bad time."

"The worst," Gomez said genially. "Please do come in."

Margaux held out the welcome basket she'd brought with her. It contained a selection of her very own line of jams and a copy of her book, *You're Welcome in Advance: The Margaux Needler Story*. Morticia stared at the basket, then donned a pair of asbestos safety gloves and gingerly took it from Margaux. She quickly passed it along to a—

A disembodied hand? Margaux stared in horror as the . . . hand took the basket and scuttled away, using its fingers as legs.

This appointment could not be over soon enough.

"Are you ready for your Margaux makeover?" she

asked, pasting her best television smile back on her face.

"Quite," Morticia said unenthusiastically. "Pugsley has been climbing the walls in anticipation." She pointed one black-polished finger, and Margaux looked over to the other side of the entryway. The young man was indeed literally crawling up the wall . . . backward. She shuddered.

Eyes on the prize, Margaux, she reminded herself. *You're here on a mission. Do it and get out of here.*

"Well," she said. "Let's take a look around, shall we? And before you say anything"—she winked at the camera—"*you're welcome.*"

Gomez and Morticia led Margaux and her crew into the dining room. She looked around. The walls were stone. Medieval sconces with torches burning in them lit the room. Everything was covered with dust and cobwebs.

Time to get to work.

"Okay!" Margaux chirped. "Now, if we're trying for a more *contemporary* look, these sconces have *got* to go." She reached out and yanked on one. The brackets didn't look all that sturdy. But instead of crumbling off the wall, the sconce slid down an inch, and something in the wall went *click*. Margaux had triggered a hidden mechanism. One of the walls rotated on a hidden hinge, swallowing a cameraman.

"Mitch?" said one of the other camera operators, but

he was gone. The wall was smooth and stationary again.

"Hmm," Morticia said regretfully. "The sconces were a gift from dead relatives."

Gomez nodded. "If we get rid of them, they'll be terribly hurt the next time they visit."

Outside, Parker had packed in her livestream and sat down under a tree. This had been fun at first, but there wasn't all that much going on in the yard, and now she was just bored. She scrolled idly through a gallery of cute kitten photos online and wondered when her mom would be ready to go.

A hand closed in and yanked her phone away. No, not a hand—a twig. What?!

Parker looked up, startled. The *tree* had taken her phone away and was handing it to—a girl Parker's age. This must be Wednesday Addams. She was wearing an old-fashioned dress, and her hair was in two severe braids. She stared at Parker, then down at the phone, which was now playing a video of Parker's favorite K-pop star in concert. The phone made a tinny roar as the video showed thousands of screaming fans cheering in the stands.

"How do all these people fit into that little contraption?" Wednesday asked. The tree wrapped a branch around Parker's waist and hoisted her onto the branch beside Wednesday.

"Eek!" Parker squeaked out.

Wednesday didn't seem to notice. "My vanity mirror only imprisons fourteen souls at a time," she added. "The witchcraft in this device is very impressive."

Parker tilted her head. "Wait," she said, "you don't have a cell phone? That's pretty weird."

Wednesday shrugged. "I may not have a . . . 'cell phone'," she replied, "but you don't seem to have a cross-bow, and I thought *everybody* had one of those."

She twirled a dangerous-looking crossbow in the hand that wasn't holding Parker's phone. Parker sort of wished she were still livestreaming. This really was too weird to be believed.

"My name is Wednesday," the girl added. Parker decided not to tell her that she knew that already. She wasn't sure how this girl would feel about learning that Margaux Needler had CIA-style dossiers compiled on the entire family and had forced her crew—and her daughter—to review and memorize them on the way there that morning.

"I'm Parker," Parker said. She looked around. "How long have you lived here?"

"My whole life," Wednesday replied. "Which seems *endless*." She struck a tragic pose.

"How come I've never seen you at school?" Parker asked.

"I'm cage-schooled," Wednesday replied.

Parker squinted, confused. "Excuse me?" she said.

"It's terribly dull," Wednesday added, "but Mother insists. She doesn't trust the outside world."

Wednesday gave Parker a sharp look. "And she doesn't trust *normal people*." Then she shrugged. "I'm actually cutting cage right now," she said. She pointed toward the house. The monster butler was carrying a large cage toward the house, and the little boy—Wednesday's brother—was inside it, growling, snarling, and tumbling himself around.

Parker's head was spinning. "Okay," she said. It wasn't okay. But she didn't know what else to say.

"So," Wednesday said curiously, "what happens at *your* school?"

Parker scratched her head. "Uh," she said, "not much, I guess. Just friends turning on each other, girls making other girls feel bad about themselves. Typical junior high stuff."

Wednesday nodded. "Intriguing," she said. "It sounds like *Richard III*, but bloodier." She cocked her head. "Can *anyone* go to your school?" she asked.

Parker shrugged. "I guess so," she said. "But who'd want to?"

Inside the house, the tour continued.

Gomez and Morticia led Margaux and her crew into the cellar. Margaux tried not to wonder when they were going to be shown the crypt . . . and locked inside. Given how things had gone so far, it didn't seem that far-fetched.

"And this is our whine cellar," Morticia said proudly, gesturing around her. "We have a lovely collection of whines."

She uncorked a bottle, and a high, sad whine emerged from it.

The tour continued. They made their way past barrels of whine and shelves of preserved . . . things until they reached what appeared to be a giant hole in the floor.

"And this is our bottomless pit," Morticia said, gesturing at it.

"How do we get across?" Margaux asked.

"One moment," Morticia said, and gave the hem of her dress a demure little shake. Thousands of spiders streamed out from under her dress and linked up to make a bridge across the pit. Margaux held her breath and tried very hard not to think about what was happening as she crossed the pit. The moment everyone was on the other side, the spiders all swarmed up to Morticia's dress and disappeared again.

"About the pit," Margaux said. "You really should consider converting it to an infinity pool. It'll raise your home equity like you would *not* believe, and they're great for entertaining."

Morticia smiled noncommittally. "Noted," she said, and the tour continued.

When the tour of the Addamses' house was over, they reconvened in the living room. Margaux smiled. It was her move now—and she knew exactly what she needed to do.

"This is fantastic!" she said brightly to Morticia, and then she turned to the cameras. "There really isn't much to do to make this place *perfect*."

She took out a can of spray paint and gave it a business-like shake.

"All we have to do is pull down these sidewalls," she said, painting giant red Xs on the walls (which she was certain were structural and load-bearing). "And then we also break down these other two walls," she added, painting big red Xs through the two exterior walls.

"And *definitely* do some demo on *this*," she said,

painting a big red X across the monster butler, whose name, evidently, was Lurch. "He's *so* nineties," she added. "*Really* out of date."

Margaux looked around thoughtfully. "Open up the ceiling," she said, looking up. She climbed up onto a table and spray-painted a giant X onto the ceiling. "Just break it. Irreversibly."

She climbed back down and rolled up the ancient Persian carpet on the floor. "And just get this nasty old floor out of the way," she added, painting a big X across the floorboards.

Margaux stood up and dusted her pants off. She looked around cheerfully. "And there you go!" she said cheerfully. The room was completely trashed. Wobbly red Xs adorned every surface. The butler had one across his face. Morticia and Gomez were looking around in shock.

Margaux felt pretty good about the whole situation. Either the Addamses would be furious at her for defacing their living room, or they'd be stupid enough to actually take her advice. And if they *did*, that would be the end of their house. The second they removed any wall from this room, the entire house would collapse. Margaux had been in the renovation business long enough to know that.

Either way, the family was going to have to move out.

Even if they didn't take her advice, there was no way they were going to stay in the area. Nobody sane would stay in a neighborhood where their most powerful neighbor was a spray-paint-wielding maniac.

Margaux grinned and raised her can of spray paint once more.

"Stop right there!" Morticia's voice rang out with such urgency that Margaux *did* stop, in spite of herself.

Morticia glided over to Margaux and took her wrist in one surprisingly strong little hand. "Don't touch another thing," she said.

Gomez hurried over. "It's perfect," Morticia said breathlessly, staring around her with starry eyes. Gomez nodded eagerly. "Ms. Needler," he said, "you have a gift."

Margaux shrugged modestly. That answered that. So they were morons and they were going to actually take her rubbish advice. That was okay with her.

"I'm so glad we agree," she said cheerfully. "I can have my makeover crew up here and swinging hammers first thing in the morning. We'll get rid of these pesky walls . . . and ceilings . . . and floors . . . for you, pronto!" She grinned at the Addamses. "What do you say?"

Gomez and Morticia exchanged confused looks. "No, no," Gomez said. He gestured at the defaced walls. "We thought you were finished!"

"We love it *just the way it is*," Morticia said serenely. "You're as good as they say."

Margaux fought the urge to scream.

"I'm so glad you like it," she said tightly. "But I really think you—"

"Our whole family is coming in two weeks," Gomez went on obliviously. "It's our son's Mazurka—you understand how it is."

Margaux's blood ran cold. "I'm sorry," she said slowly, "*two weeks*, you say?"

Glenn hissed at her from behind the wall of camera operators. "Our finale is in two weeks!"

Margaux glared at him. "*Thank you, Glenn*," she hissed back.

"It's a gracious offer, Ms. Needler," Morticia said firmly. "But you really have done enough. We're so grateful."

Morticia and Gomez escorted Margaux and her crew out of the house. Margaux's head was spinning . . . and now, finally, she was really panicking.

"Gomez," she said, clutching at his suit sleeve. "I can call you Gomez, right? I feel like we have a connection. Anyway," she hurried on, not waiting for him to respond,

"Gomez, I'll be blunt: I have fifty houses to sell down there in Eastfield Estates." She pointed down the hill toward the little burgh, where even now a brand-new golf course was being installed. "And the view those houses have of your property, well . . ."

Gomez smiled widely at her. Margaux hurried on. "Well, Gomez, it's *off-brand* for my . . . uh, brand."

"Fifty houses, you say?" Gomez asked.

"Yes," Margaux said urgently, "And you need to understand that—"

But Gomez interrupted her with a misty look in his eye. "You should know, Ms. Needler," he said gently, "that ever since my family was chased from the old country, my *one dream* has been to find a place we could call home. Once they see Eastfield Estates, I think they'll want to stay for good. This is a lovely opportunity. The best. You're a dream come true. Thank you so much for coming by. Please don't let the gate eat you on your way out."

"Thanks, you too," Margaux said automatically, her head spinning, as Gomez gently hurried her down the path toward the gate at the bottom of the grounds. "Wait, what?"

"Run!" Gomez called. "Run, Margaux, run! I'll distract it! Run!"

Gomez threw a raw steak at the wrought iron gate, which greedily chomped down on the treat. Margaux and her team fled through while it was distracted and came to a stop at a safe distance. Margaux watched the gate finish eating the steak, her eyes wide with horror. She'd never seen a gate eat *anything* before.

Parker was leaning against a tree nearby, looking at her phone.

"That Wednesday girl is a freak," Parker said, not looking up. "I like her."

Glenn turned to Margaux. "We're about to be invaded by a whole *army* of freaks," he said urgently. "What are we gonna do about the finale, Margaux?!"

Margaux had caught her breath by now. She wasn't beat. Not by a long shot. She looked back up at the hideous house looming at the top of the hill.

"It's tragic when people can't accept the help they so badly need," she said. "And when that happens . . ."

She locked eyes with Glenn. "Another kind of intervention is needed," she finished ominously.

CHAPTER 6

Back in the house, Gomez and Morticia discussed the situation.

"I agree, Gomez," Morticia said as she knitted. "The whole family moving here would be a dream come true. But," she added, looking up, "I don't trust that Margaux woman."

Gomez was poking through the welcome basket that Margaux had brought. "She's an eccentric, darling," he said. "Give her a chance." He pulled a jar of something out of the basket. "Raspberry preserves," he read, puzzled.

"Never heard of it. Must be some kind of scented embalming fluid."

Morticia raised an eyebrow. That *was* a very neighborly gift. Maybe she'd been wrong about Margaux.

"Gah!" Gomez said, starting violently. Wednesday had appeared behind him, apparently out of nowhere.

"Wednesday," Morticia scolded gently. "I've told you a thousand times. Practice your lurking on someone other than your father. He's just too easy."

"Yes, Mother," a voice in Morticia's ear said softly. She did *not* jump, but it took some willpower. "Better," Morticia said approvingly. She looked up at Wednesday— who was now standing behind the couch—and smiled. Wednesday smiled back and climbed over the couch to sit down next to her mother.

Gomez came over as well. "What's on your mind, my little nightcrawler?" he asked.

Wednesday looked down at her hands, which were clasped in her lap. "Well," she said, "I spoke with Parker this afternoon. She's the daughter of that talking mannequin who came to visit."

Morticia looked up from her knitting. "I wasn't aware that Margaux had a daughter," she said. "What did you talk about?"

"She told me about a communal school all the neighborhood children attend," Wednesday said. "It's called . . . *junior high*."

Morticia shivered. It sounded awful to her.

Gomez nodded. "*Junior high*," he repeated, his voice grave. "I've read about those in my abnormal psychology books."

Wednesday went on, her voice small but determined. "Anyone of age can enroll," she said. Morticia felt her heart sinking. But she didn't let anything show on her face. "I think," Wednesday added, "that it would be . . . *good* for me."

A long, long, silent moment went by. Morticia knitted and knitted and did not look at Wednesday.

Gomez cleared his throat. "I think it's a capital idea!" he said.

Morticia came to the end of one row of stitches and began the next. "And what of your studies here?" she asked calmly, still not looking up. "Your taxidermy is coming along so well."

Wednesday sighed impatiently. "Mother," she said, "would you really deprive me of the opportunity to torment children my own age?"

"She makes a point," Gomez chimed in. "What's more,

with Wednesday in school, we'd get to know the people here even better!"

"Well, Mother?" Wednesday asked eagerly.

Morticia looked up at last. She looked at her husband, his eager, cheerful face. She looked at her daughter, her anxious, pinched, sweet little snout.

She was outnumbered.

Eastfield Estates Middle School was a tidy, cheerful building. It had an Olympic-sized swimming pool and an award-winning science club. The cafeteria served quinoa on Tuesdays and Thursdays. It was everything a devoted parent could want for their child.

Gomez stared at the building with profound disappointment. "I've *heard* public schools are filthy, dangerous places," he muttered, "but I'm just not seeing it." He'd had such high hopes, but they were all dashed by the reality. It was so tidy. So cheerful. Gomez sighed.

But Wednesday seemed unfazed. She strode confidently into the building, not even pausing to wave goodbye to her family.

What neither Gomez nor Wednesday noticed was that the crossing guard waving kids across the street was staring intently at Wednesday. He spoke into a radio in a hushed voice. "The snail is on the turtle's back," he said. "I repeat, the snail is on the turtle's back."

Margaux Needler's voice replied over the radio, tinny and staticky. "Glenn, what the heck are you talking about?"

Glenn (the crossing guard was indeed Glenn in disguise) sighed. So much for the cloak-and-dagger approach. "Wednesday Addams is entering the school," he translated.

"Looks like the game is on," Margaux murmured. She clipped her walkie-talkie back onto her belt and strode into her "craft room." It was a glorified closet lined with tidy shelves of crafting gear. Margaux pulled a wrapping-paper tube away from the wall, and the floor began to lower slowly into a secret basement lair.

This was Margaux's secret office and base of operations.

She sat down in front of a computer and pulled up the Neighborhood Peeps website. It was a social media site for neighborhood busybodies, and it was the cornerstone of Margaux's new anti-Addams plan.

She cracked her knuckles and started typing. "Let's see," Margaux muttered. "Who shall I be today?" She scrolled through all the fake accounts she'd set up for the site. "How about Shelly Longbottom, on Sugar Ridge Lane?"

She clicked into "Shelly's" account and typed furiously.

Did you hear about those Addams people? Someone told me they're wanted in thirty states.

She hit "post." Then Margaux clicked into another fake account. "And from Robert Gently on Gigglemountain Way . . ." she murmured.

. . . I hear they're training wild animals to steal our children.

Margaux hit "post" and giggled happily. On to the next one.

Throughout Eastfield Estates, townspeople's smartphones started chiming.

"Those Addams people are growing a garden of man-eating plants?" one villager said, staring at the message that had popped up on her phone.

"Their butler broke a man in half?" another whispered.

"Where are they from, anyway?" a waitress in a café demanded, staring at her phone while she refilled a cup of coffee.

"Doesn't matter," the cook replied, staring at his own phone while he flipped a frypan full of flapjacks. "It's obvious they don't belong here."

"We need to talk to Margaux!" several of the patrons in the café all cried, staring at their phones in dismay.

Wednesday looked around thoughtfully as she entered the building. So this was a "school." As she entered the lobby, all the kids went silent and stared. They'd never seen anyone like Wednesday before in their entire lives.

"Ah," Wednesday said, looking around and taking everything in. The security guard at the door. The bars on the windows. The closed-circuit cameras. "Now I understand. This is a children's prison."

She spotted Parker talking to some other girls their age by the lockers and walked over to join them.

"Oh boy," Parker said. "Guys, this is Wednesday."

Wednesday smiled. It was her best middle-school-girl smile. But that doesn't mean it was any good.

"Hello," she said, smiling and smiling.

The girls took a nervous step back.

Another girl, this one with a mean look on her face, walked by the group of girls. She grabbed Parker's backpack and shoved something into it. "Hey, Parker," she said, sneering, "I got something for you." She handed the backpack back to Parker, who peered inside. She sighed.

"A moldy sandwich, Bethany?" Parker said. "You're slipping."

"You know what, you're right," Bethany replied nastily. "Let's kick it up a notch."

She grabbed a big cup of soda from one of Parker's friends and poured it into the backpack. Then she closed the backpack and shook it up. It started foaming alarmingly as Bethany handed it back to Parker.

"Can't you take a joke, Parker?" Bethany asked. "You have no sense of humor." She smiled sweetly and turned to go.

"Bethany, is it?" Wednesday said. Bethany stopped in her tracks and turned around. "Don't cut your eyes on my crew unless you're ready to dance," Wednesday said coldly.

Bethany paused, and then turned again and walked away. "Whatever," she said as she left.

"What did you do?" one of Parker's friends said anxiously.

"You shouldn't have said that," another added.

"There's nothing you can do," Parker told Wednesday gloomily. "Bethany is way too popular."

"Popularity is fleeting," Wednesday said. "I prefer to set my sights on something a little more challenging."

All three girls stared at Wednesday in fascination. "Like what?" they said in unison.

Wednesday reached into Parker's backpack, grabbed the moldy (and soda-soaked) sandwich, and took a bite.

"Vigilante justice," she said.

Wednesday wasn't sure about this whole *school* thing until she got to fourth period. Fourth period was science class. And apparently science class meant—

"Ew," Parker's friend Layla said. "Dead frogs."

"I don't think I can do this," Parker's friend Kayla said.

"Yuck," Parker said.

Each student had a dead frog on a little plastic tray in front of them.

"Oh," Wednesday said. Finally, she knew what was going on. "I've done this thousands of times."

All the kids stopped what they were doing and watched as Wednesday went to work. She pulled parts and equipment from all corners of the room until she had a complicated battery system rigged up.

Wednesday held the two electrodes and carefully touched them to either side of her dead frog's chest. "Flip the switch!" she commanded Parker. Parker shoved her goggles down over her eyes and obeyed.

Electricity pulsed. There was a loud hum, and lightning arced across the room.

"Give my creature life!" Wednesday yelled, struggling to hold the electrodes steady as the frog's body twitched and jumped. "Live! Live, I tell you! LIVE!"

The frog gasped, and its eyes flew open.

"It's alive!" Parker shrieked.

Wednesday whooped with excitement, and then—

Electricity arced from her frog to the one next to it, and from that frog to the next, and soon every dead frog in the science classroom was a living zombie frog.

They all turned and looked to Wednesday for instructions. She silently pointed at Bethany, who stood, stunned, surrounded by frogs. Then, all at once the frogs leapt at her face.

Bethany fled, screaming, covered in frogs.

Wednesday watched her go. Then she turned to her new friends. "Bethany's really changed her look," she observed. "It suits her."

Parker burst out laughing.

"It's an honor," Layla started.

"And a privilege," Kayla continued.

"To watch you work," they finished in unison.

"Hey, you wanna go to the mall?" Parker asked,

slinging an arm around Wednesday.

"Sure," Wednesday said. "Why not? I haven't seen a good mauling in ages."

Morticia stared anxiously out the window. The sun had nearly set, and Wednesday was still not home.

"It's late," she said to Gomez. "I'm worried."

"Darling," Gomez said soothingly. "Wednesday will be fine. She can take care of herself."

Morticia shook her head. "Oh, no," she said, "it's not Wednesday I'm worried about. It's the rest of them." She looked out the window again. "We may need to provide an alibi."

"My love," Gomez said. He was standing on his head in the parlor. "It's game night. Wednesday will be home soon, so why don't you come and join us?"

Morticia sighed and sat down. She examined the game board.

"Oh, very well," she said. "F-6?"

Gomez chortled. "Pugsley!" he cried. "You heard your mother! Blow F-6!"

Pugsley sat at a naval sonar control panel, fiddling with various dials. He straightened up and turned a key to unlock a bulletproof plastic dome over a big red button.

"Fire in the hole!" he yelled, and punched the button as hard as he could.

Upstairs, Uncle Fester was in the bathtub, playing with a toy battleship floatie.

"I'm the king of the world!" he said cheerfully.

KABLAMMO!

The battleship toy blew up in a massive explosion. The floor of the bathroom gave way, and the bathtub—with Uncle Fester in it—fell straight through the floor, slamming into the parlor. Water sloshed out onto the Persian carpet.

"Yes!" Pugsley said, throwing his hands in the air triumphantly.

"You sunk my ship!" Fester chirped.

"Well done, Pugsley!" Gomez said approvingly. Pugsley blushed happily.

Just then, a rumbling sounded from the fireplace. A crystal ball fell from the chimney and rolled across the carpet. Then a carpet bag fell into the fire grate with a *thump*, followed by something large that landed in an explosion of ash. When the ash finally cleared, Morticia made out a grimy figure climbing to her feet in front of the fireplace.

"Hello, my uglies!" the figure croaked. She shook herself hard, and another layer of ash fell away.

"Oh goodness," Morticia said softly. It was Grandma.

"Mother!" Gomez exclaimed, springing up from his armchair. "I thought I felt my skin crawling!" He hurried over and embraced her.

"Grandma," Morticia said carefully. "What a surprise. The Mazurka isn't until next week. Why are you here so early?"

Grandma shrugged. "Gomez said you needed help with the party," she said.

Morticia glared at Gomez. "It's true!" he said cheerfully. "I sent for her!"

"I can't believe," Morticia said, smiling through her teeth, "that you *bothered your mother with that, darling.*"

Gomez looked up, hearing the fury behind her smile. He gulped nervously. "Neither . . . can I?" he said. He clearly recognized his mistake now, when it was too late to do anything about it.

"He said you were in over your head," Grandma said, cheerfully patting Morticia's arm.

"Thank you, Mother!" Gomez said, making a "please stop talking" motion with his hand. She didn't notice.

"He said he wasn't sure if you were up to the challenge," she went on. Morticia's eyes went wide with fury.

"I didn't say that, exactly," Gomez said weakly.

"You did!" Grandma said earnestly. "That's exactly what you said! And you also said—"

"You know what?" Gomez said, interrupting her. "I'm starving. Let's eat!"

Morticia shook her head. "Not until Wednesday gets home."

Grandma perked up. "Where *is* that granddaughter of mine?" she asked. "I've got something for her!" She held up a bear trap.

Bang! The front door slammed open. Wednesday strode straight through the foyer toward the stairs without even looking at her parents.

"Wednesday?" Morticia called. "Where have you been?"

"Elsewhere," Wednesday said shortly. She turned to face her mother.

Morticia gasped.

There was a brightly colored barrette in Wednesday's hair.

Shakily, Morticia made her way over to Wednesday.

"What," Morticia said, reaching a trembling hand up to the piece of plastic clipped into Wednesday's hair, "is that."

"Parker calls it a 'pop of color,'" Wednesday said casually.

Morticia swallowed hard and did her best to keep her voice level. "I see," she said.

"She says it brings out my smile," Wednesday went on.

"Wednesday," Morticia said evenly, "you don't *have* a smile."

"Turns out I have lots of things you don't know about," Wednesday said tartly. She marched upstairs without another word. Morticia watched her go in stunned silence.

"I see I got here just in time," Grandma said. "You were right to call, Gomez."

Morticia whirled around. "Thank you, Grandma," she said. "But I'll handle this myself."

She glided up the stairs and entered Wednesday's room.

"Wednesday?" she said, sitting down on the bed and watching as Wednesday chopped the heads off a row of dolls. *At least she is engaging in normal, healthy play,* Morticia thought. *Perhaps this barrette business is a red herring. Still . . .*

"How would you like to join me tomorrow after your 'school,' for tea and a séance in the cemetery?" she asked.

Wednesday glowered and didn't look up. "If you like, Mother," she said sullenly. She pulled out a stiletto blade and threw it in Morticia's direction. It whizzed just past Morticia's ear and hit the light switch, turning it off.

Morticia knew when she wasn't welcome.

"Sleep well, dear," she said. She closed the door behind her and heaved a big sigh.

Her little girl was growing up and discovering things like . . . *wholesomeness*. And *fun*.

Morticia had always known this day would come.

But that didn't make it any easier.

The next afternoon, Morticia boiled water for tea and set up a charming little table in the cemetery. She put out the Ouija board and a small bowl of sugar cubes. A crystal ball went next to the teapot, and Morticia settled in with a hot cup of pekoe.

Right on time, the crystal ball gave a cheery ring like a telephone. Morticia carefully moved the piece across the Ouija board to the "yes" space, and a ghostly face appeared in the surface of the crystal ball.

"Hello, Mother," Morticia said, smiling.

"Where's my little wraith?" Grandma Frump said, peering left and right.

Morticia sighed. "Wednesday still hasn't arrived," she said. "It seems she's stood us up."

"What do you mean?" Grandma Frump said, frowning in the crystal ball.

"I think she's distancing herself from me," Morticia said. "The world can be so cruel. I'm afraid it's going to change her, but all she wants to do is run toward it."

Grandma Frump tilted her head. "She's a lot like you that way," she said. "You were always looking for something outside of what we gave you."

Grandpa Frump's face appeared in the crystal ball. "Let me talk to her," he said. "Listen, Morticia," he went on, "life is life. How do you think we felt about leaving you behind? We felt helpless. But we knew you'd be okay. We raised you to be strong."

Morticia's eyes filled with tears. "Wednesday's growing up," Grandpa Frump went on. "Trust your daughter. She'll find her way."

Morticia smiled a watery smile. "Thank you, Father," she said. "That's most comforting."

Her father smiled back through the crystal ball. "Good," he said.

Meanwhile, in Parker's bedroom, in a brand-new house down in Eastfield Estates, Wednesday and Parker were hanging out. Wednesday was using a magnifying glass and sunlight to burn out the eyes of a teen heartthrob on the cover of a glossy magazine. Parker was poking at the photo app on her phone.

"You know," Parker said, "when I met you, I thought you were super weird. But now I think you're really cool."

"Same," Wednesday said.

"Oh!" Parker said, sitting up. "How'd that barrette go over at home yesterday?"

Wednesday frowned. "It was odd. My mother was . . . accepting. It depressed me. One never wants to see one's mother that way. Accepting. Mothers should be terrifying gorgons—unreasonable and unappeasable."

Wednesday smiled. "But I must admit," she went on, "walking around in something so garish . . . so grotesque . . . I was shocked at how thrilling it felt."

Parker sighed. "I wish I could do that," she said. "But my mom makes me wear this preppy stuff, and I just hate it. I would love to wear something that would really *shock* her."

Wednesday grinned. "Well, Parker," she said, "you're in luck. I'm the *queen* of shock."

Morticia gritted her teeth and smiled. "Thank you very much," she said to the barbershop quartet of four shrunken heads on a platter. They'd just finished singing an audition tune for her.

The heads all grinned and blinked in unison. "Our pleasure!" they chorused.

Morticia sighed and turned to Grandma Addams. "Grandma," she said patiently, "we already *have* a band for Pugsley's Mazurka. They came highly recommended from the mortuary. I'm not sure why you think we should be trying out other bands."

Grandma smiled. "Oh, I'm sure *your* band is just *fine*," she said reassuringly. "But my sister Sloom is going to be judging Pugsley. And if things aren't done the traditional way, she won't be happy—and the Mazurka will be a disaster."

Then she sighed. "But what do I know," she added.

Morticia knew when she was beat. "Fine," she said shortly. A distant *bang* sounded from the front of the house. The front door. "Excuse me," Morticia said. "I'd better go and see who it is."

She rounded a corner into the living room and stopped short. Wednesday was there dressed in a pink polo shirt and khaki shorts.

Morticia clutched her chest and gasped.

Wednesday opened her mouth and began to sing.

"What's so great about being yourself, when you can be like everyone else?"

Morticia gathered her wits enough to speak. "How *dare* you enter this house looking like that," she said sharply. "Where have you *been*?"

Wednesday shrugged. "Hanging out with Parker."

Grandma Addams stepped into the room and stared. "Holy Hades!" she exclaimed.

"Do you like my new look," Wednesday said. It was less of a question and more of a statement.

"I do *not* like it," Morticia said sharply. "Everyone knows pink is a gateway color."

Grandma poked Morticia. "I warned you about sending her to public school," she muttered.

"Don't worry," Morticia snapped back, not taking her eyes away from Wednesday, "Wednesday is never going to that school again."

Wednesday gasped. *"What?!"* she said.

"In fact," Morticia went on furiously, "she's never leaving this *house* again!"

Wednesday stormed up to her room.

Things didn't go much better for Parker.

She had shaved her head. She was wearing heavy goth makeup. She'd dyed all her clothes black and shredded holes in half of them.

She'd never felt so *free*. "I'm living my truth," she announced on her video stream, angling her head this way and that so her followers could see her new piercings, her new eyeliner, and her new (lack of) hair. She had closed the shades so her room was appropriately gloomy, but it did make it kind of hard to get a good picture on video. Parker considered turning on a light but then decided that that would betray her new goth identity. Her followers would just have to deal with dark video from now on.

"*YEAHHHHGHH!*"

A shrill scream pierced the air, and Parker hastily ended the stream and put her phone down. Her mother was standing in her bedroom doorway, staring at her in shock and fury.

"*Parker?*" she screamed. "Who *did* this to you?!"

Stay strong, Parker reminded herself. *She's not the boss of you.*

"I did this," she said solemnly. "This is my new look, Mother. I choose my clothes from now on, not you."

Margaux clenched her fists . . . and her jaw.

"This is that little creep Wednesday Addams's work, isn't it," she spat out from between her teeth.

Parker sighed and shook her head. "She's not a creep, Mother. She's just not like *you*."

Margaux opened her mouth to retort, but Parker cut her off.

"Why can't you ever let people be *different*?" she asked. All her life, Parker had put up with her mother's attempts to make her fit in. She'd worn the clothes her mother chose. She'd worn her hair the way her mother wanted. She'd even studied the French horn. Ugh.

Well, no more.

"Because," Margaux hissed, "it's my *calling* to make everyone the same. It is *literally my job, Parker*."

She bent down until her face was right in Parker's face and locked eyes with her. "And if they can't accept my help, then they don't belong in Eastfield Estates."

Margaux straightened up and briskly walked over to the light switch and flicked on the lights.

"Augh!" Parker shrieked. "Too bright! It burns!" The light stabbed her eyeballs. She was a goth now, and that meant *no light*. Why couldn't her mother just accept that?

"Good," Margaux said harshly. "Maybe it'll burn away the weird."

Parker jumped up off her bed. "I *hate* it here!" she shrieked. "Everything's boring and fake and bright. Like *plastic flowers*. Like *you*!"

Margaux drew herself up, outraged. "Parker!" she

shouted back. "Plastic flowers live forever! Now you think long and hard about that . . . with *no social media*."

She ripped Parker's phone out of her hand.

"No!" Parker cried, scrabbling desperately at Margaux's fist. "Not that! Anything but that!" But Margaux turned and walked off, taking Parker's phone with her.

Parker threw herself on her bed face-first. She *hated* her mom. And she *hated* this town.

Margaux threw herself into her secret lair. She *hated* the Addamses. And she *hated* what they were doing to her perfect town. What they were doing to her perfect daughter.

Nobody knew about the lair beneath Margaux's craft room—not even Parker. But it was the nerve center of Margaux's entire operation. Here she had computers and monitors—all the equipment she needed to keep her perfect town . . . perfect. Here was where she did her best thinking, her best scheming. Here was where she was in charge. Where she knew exactly what to do.

Margaux took a deep breath. She knew what her next move was. She slid Parker's phone into her pocket and went over to her computer. She logged onto Neighborhood Peeps and began reading through the recent conversations in Eastfield Estates. Margaux smiled when she saw that the fake rumors she'd planted had taken off. There was already plenty of alarm about the Addamses.

"It's obvious they don't belong here," one said.

"We should *do* something," said another.

"I'm worried for our children," said a third.

Margaux smiled. The neighborhood was already on the verge of rising up against the unwanted weirdos. All she needed to do now was fan the flames a little more.

She cracked her knuckles and started typing.

CHAPTER 7

A record played on a turntable, polluting the night with its hideous, scratchy, discordant music.

Uneven, stumbling footsteps rang through the Addamses' house—*clomp a-clomp clomp.*

Morticia, knitting an unspeakable monstrosity of a sweater in the parlor, looked up as plaster dust sifted down from the ceiling. She smiled.

Pugsley was practicing the Sabre Mazurka.

Upstairs, Pugsley wheezed and sweated as he stumbled through the steps. He paused and shook his head. Was he getting *worse*? It felt like he was getting worse.

Something flashed by his window, and he turned to stare into the darkness. What was out there?

"Aagh!" Pugsley yelled as Wednesday's face appeared in his window. She stared blankly at him and then dropped out of sight. He ran to the window and opened it, staring out.

Wednesday, borne by Ichabod the tree, was descending from her window to the ground. She was carrying a bag.

"Where are you going?" Pugsley asked her. Ichabod paused, and Wednesday hung in the air in front of Pugsley's window.

"A friend's," Wednesday answered shortly. She shouldered her bag. "*I* hold people prisoner, not the other way around. Good luck with your Mazurka. You need it."

Ichabod began to lower her toward the ground.

"Wait," Pugsley called, and Ichabod paused again. "You're leaving? Who's gonna torment me every day?"

Wednesday sighed impatiently. "Living under this roof is all the torment you'll need. Besides, our parents have made it clear to me that the only way to be accepted in this family is to be exactly like them. I thought the Addamses valued difference, but I guess not. I can't play by these rules anymore."

Wednesday looked at Pugsley. "Farewell, brother,"

she said. "Tomorrow you become a man. And tonight I become a fugitive."

Pugsley thought this over, then shrugged. "I always kinda knew it'd end up like this. I just didn't think it'd be so soon."

Wednesday nodded. Then Ichabod lowered her completely out of sight.

She was gone.

"Pugsley," a voice murmured from the trap door to his bedroom. Pugsley jumped and slammed his head on the window sill.

"Have you seen your sister?" his mother asked, gliding into the room. "She's not in her room."

Pugsley rubbed his head and stared nervously at her. She had ways of making you talk—Pugsley knew this from long, hard experience.

"Pugsley," Morticia murmured, staring him intensely in the face. "Where is Wednesday."

Pugsley squirmed. He was going to crack soon, he knew it. Desperate times called for desperate measures— maybe he could hypnotize his mother before she could pry it out of him. He had to try!

He whipped out a watch on a chain and set it rocking back and forth like a pendulum.

"*You're getting very sleepy . . .*" he said uncertainly, trying to make his voice soothing and hypnotic.

"Pugsley," Morticia said, drawing closer. She did not look amused. Pugsley's heart started pounding. He was going to screw this up somehow, he just knew it.

"*She did not go to her friend's house . . .*" he said, still trying for a hypnotic voice.

Morticia's gaze sharpened. "She went to her friend's house?"

Pugsley swallowed. "*I repeat,*" he said, swinging the pendulum faster and faster, "*she did not go to her friend's house.*"

Morticia looked out Pugsley's window into the dark night. Pugsley winced and braced himself for an eruption. But Morticia just stood there for a moment longer, and then sighed, slumping a little. She looked . . . *sad.* And somehow that was worse than any scolding.

She straightened up and pasted a serene look onto her face, but Pugsley wasn't fooled. He could tell she was really, really sad. He watched his mother glide out of his room, her head high and her back straight. He felt heartsore just looking at her.

Pugsley sighed and plopped back down on his bed. He didn't feel like practicing the Mazurka anymore. Not that he had felt like it before. He was terrible at it, and he knew it. The only thing he had a real talent for was explosives. He had no idea what to do with a *sword*.

He pulled a photo album onto his lap and opened it up, turning the pages slowly. It was the album of his father's Sabre Mazurka. Gomez had lent it to Pugsley to help motivate him. But it had the opposite effect. Looking at the photos of his father as a kid . . . Gomez was so graceful, so confident. He held the sword like it was an extension of himself. He was smiling in every photo.

Plop! A drop of water fell onto one of the photos. Pugsley jumped and gently wiped the water off. He sniffled and wiped his eyes. When had he started crying?

He sniffled again. His Mazurka was going to be a disaster, and there was nothing he could do. His sister was gone. His mother was heartbroken. His entire extended family was going to watch him fail tomorrow.

And his father was going to be *so disappointed in him*.

Pugsley tilted over and fell sideways onto his bed. He buried his face in his pillow and cried himself to sleep.

The next morning, the sun rose into a cloudless blue sky. It was perfect weather for the season finale of *Design Intervention*.

Glenn checked his checklist, then another checklist, then double-checked the checklist of checklists.

"Check," he muttered to himself. He was ready.

He strode out into the town square, where the crew for the live broadcast had assembled. About thirty locals from Eastfield Estates had gathered as well—extras to add some cheerful crowd scenes to the show.

"Okay, everyone!" Glenn said. "Listen up. We're going to shoot across the town square to the gazebo, where Margaux will make her grand entrance. So everyone will be walking in this direction across the square." He gestured to the crowd of locals. "Judy, you start here." He grabbed a middle-aged man and walked him over to the sidewalk, where he positioned him facing east. "Ken, you're going to follow Judy—"

Hmm. For this shot, Glenn really wanted one more local person to liven things up. Without looking carefully, he tugged another woman out of the crowd of Eastfield Estates locals and pulled her toward Ken and Judy.

"And you can stand right here," he started, and then stopped and stared.

The woman he'd chosen had a towering bouffant hairdo, and there was . . .

There was a man's head sticking out of her hair.

Glenn stared at the man's head. The eyes blinked, and Glenn jumped a mile.

"Howdee do," the man said. "I'm Ggerri. I could really go for a nonfat half-caf half-sweet almond milk mocha latte. Is there a café around here, my good sir?"

Oh god. Glenn had no idea how to respond. He whirled around, and for the first time that morning, he finally noticed that about half of the crowd of "locals" were weirdos of the first order. A woman walking on her knuckles walked—er, knuckled—up to Glenn. "Is there a bathroom nearby?" she asked politely.

"Excuse me," Glenn said weakly, and then he turned and ran.

He dodged into an alley and whipped out his walkie-talkie.

"Margaux!" he squawked into the radio. "Margaux! Come in, Margaux! The cheese is in the trunk! I repeat, the cheese is in the—"

The radio crackled, and Margaux's voice cut him off. "What are you talking about?" she said impatiently.

"The Addamses' guests have arrived!" Glenn replied. "They're *here*! What should we do?!"

"What we always do, Glenn," Margaux said calmly. "*Help people.*"

* * *

In her secret office, Margaux put down her walkie-talkie
and turned to one of her computers. She opened the Neighborhood Peeps site and began typing. She hit "post" and
then stood up and left her secret office, carefully closing
the door. She was needed in town—her plan was coming
to fruition.

Margaux Needler stepped out onto the cheerful, boring, *normal* street of cheerful, boring, *normal* Eastfield
Estates and smiled.

Across Eastfield Estates, phones began chiming with
alerts. And the "normal" citizens of the town began to
march toward Margaux's house. The time had come, and
they were ready.

Up on top of the hill, extended Addams family members
were arriving for the Mazurka. The first car to pull into the
driveway was a deluxe limousine. It rolled to a stop in front
of the front door, the tires crunching gently on the gravel.

The car door opened, and a strange creature stepped
out. From his wing-tip shoes to his white cane to his dia-
mond ring, he was dressed to kill. He was also about three
feet tall and absolutely covered in hair. A small bowler hat
and a pair of sunglasses sat neatly perched over the glossy

brown hair that covered his entire body—including his face—and fell neatly to the floor.

The front door opened, and Gomez and Morticia popped out on either side of Lurch. "It!" cried Gomez. "Cousin! You made it!"

Morticia smiled graciously. "Please come in," she said, ushering It into the family's rundown mansion. "Make yourself at home."

Wednesday Addams woke up with a crick in her neck. She'd spent the night on the floor of Parker's room, cuddled up in a neon-pink sleeping bag. She wasn't sure Parker's mother even knew she was there. Parker said Margaux was so distracted by the upcoming live episode of her television show that she barely noticed the nose on her own face.

Sure enough, the house seemed to be totally empty except for Wednesday and Parker. The two girls made their way downstairs and ate a late breakfast of cereal and orange juice. Wednesday stared down at her bowl in confusion.

"You mean it's just wheat and sugar and preservatives?" she asked Parker for the fourth time.

"I guess," Parker said. "Why, what were you expecting?"

"There's no poison in it at *all*?" Wednesday continued.

"Not even trace amounts?"

"Sorry to disappoint," Parker said. "I'm pretty sure the preservatives aren't *great* for you, but I'm not sure I'd call them poison. Same goes for the sugar, honestly."

"Fascinating," Wednesday said. She slurped the milk from the bottom of her bowl. "Your life is very strange, Parker. I think I like it."

"I'm glad you do," Parker said, "because I'm beginning to think I hate it."

She reached into her pocket, only to find it empty. "Ugh," Parker said impatiently. "I wish I knew where my mom hid my phone. I haven't been on social media in forever, and it's *killing* me. I've looked everywhere."

Parker glanced down the hall. "Except my mom's craft room," she added nervously.

"Why not look there?" Wednesday asked.

Parker shivered. "*No one* is allowed in there. I've never even seen inside it. She goes in there a lot, but she always keeps the door shut."

Wednesday rolled her eyes. "Then that's where it is," she said. Parker might have some residual fear of Margaux Needler, but Wednesday didn't know the meaning of fear—literally.

She led Parker into the craft room. It was basically a

walk-in closet bursting with neatly organized crafting supplies.

"Weird," Parker said. "I always pictured it bigger."

Wednesday poked around, lifting up trays of bright thread, sorting through piles of scrapbooking stamps. It didn't really make sense. The room barely had space to stand in, and there were no windows—and no vents. Was Margaux really spending hours locked in a closet? Wednesday rifled through an umbrella stand full of tubes of wrapping paper. One of them slid toward her when she pulled on it and gave a very clear *click* as it swung.

Behind the girls, the door to the craft room swung shut. The floor gave a little shiver and then began to lower. The craft room was a secret elevator! But where did it lead? Parker grabbed Wednesday's hand, and Wednesday squeezed it comfortingly.

The floor stopped its descent with a jarring *bump*, and a wall slid away, revealing a large, underground room full of computer screens and various kinds of security equipment.

"Whoa," Parker said softly.

"Hidden depths," Wednesday said. If she didn't hate Margaux Needler so much, she'd almost be impressed: this was the kind of evil that Wednesday usually admired.

"What *is* all this?" Parker asked, walking tentatively into the room. There were dozens of computer screens, each showing a different video feed. One showed a living room where a man was reading a magazine and drinking a cup of tea. Another showed a kitchen where a couple of kids were playing a board game at the kitchen table. All around the room, computer monitors displayed live feeds from . . .

"Oh my gosh," Parker said softly. "My mom must have built hidden cameras into all of the houses when she renovated all of Eastfield."

Wednesday's eyes opened wide. "She really *is* depraved," she said with reluctant admiration.

Parker went up to one monitor and peered at it. "There's Mr. Hanley making a sandwich," she said. She moved on to the next. "And there's our science teacher! Ms. Gravely! She's putting her . . . *underwear in the freezer*?!"

Wednesday examined a different feed. "Who's that woman putting ketchup on a piece of birthday cake?" she asked.

"That's Mrs. Pickering," Parker replied. "And that guy trying to put a tiny tuxedo on his cat, that's Mr. Flynn."

A tinny yowl emerged from the video feed.

"My money's on the cat," Wednesday said.

"She's watching *every house in town*," Parker whispered.

Wednesday and Parker looked at each other.

"We have to *tell* someone," Parker said, and they turned to the elevator, then stopped short. Margaux Needler was standing in the elevator at the entrance to her secret office. She snarled, and Parker took a step back. Even Wednesday felt a moment's alarm. There was something truly unhinged about the look on Margaux's face.

"Mom," Parker said, her voice shaking. "We, uh, we were just looking for you."

"Parker," Margaux said so sweetly that her voice practically dripped with honey. "What have I told you about Mommy's crafting room?"

Margaux pushed Wednesday and Parker into the attic. The girls stumbled and tripped, turning to look at her as she loomed in the doorway.

"Sorry to do this," Margaux said sweetly, "but standards must be upheld. Parker, someday you'll understand."

She turned to Wednesday. "And Wednesday . . ." She seemed to change her mind. She shook her head and turned back to Parker. "Well, anyway, Parker, someday you'll understand."

Margaux smiled sweetly at the girls, then locked the door behind her.

Click.

Parker stomped her foot. "Ugh," she said. "My mom has a lair *and* a jail? I *knew* I should have told the judge I wanted to live with my dad."

CHAPTER 8

The extended Addamses and Frumps continued to stream up the hill and into the Addams family home. The air was noisy with excited chattering as the celebration got going in full force.

Gomez and Morticia stood at the entrance to their home, happily greeting each guest as they came in. A middle-aged woman with plants instead of hair bounded up the steps and hugged Morticia, then Gomez.

"Salutations, Addamses! We're here!" she said cheerfully.

"Cousin Petunia!" Morticia replied warmly, kissing her

on the cheek. "I love what you've done with your hair!"

Petunia patted her leaves proudly. "Thanks," she said, "I just had it mowed."

Uncle Onion was right behind her, and greeted his nephew with a big, smelly hug. Gomez's eyes immediately began to water.

"Uncle Onion," he said, sniffling, "it's been so long! I don't know why, but I just get so sentimental around you!" He blew his nose loudly.

"Don't cry," Uncle Onion said. "Then I'll start crying, and then it'll be a whole thing." His eyes were already looking rather glassy.

The guests continued to stream in, each stranger—and happier—than the last. Gomez beamed happily as he watched his family coming together for their first reunion since his marriage to Morticia. But Morticia—

Gomez frowned. Morticia didn't look as happy as he felt. And then he remembered—Wednesday.

Wednesday, who had worn a brightly colored barrette in her hair. Who had stood her mother up for a séance tea party. Who had worn a pink polo shirt and run away from home.

Wednesday, who wasn't here today to see her only brother's Sabre Mazurka. Who was missing the reunion of the entire Addams and Frump clans.

Suddenly, Gomez wasn't feeling so cheerful, either.

Morticia caught his eye. "Darling," she said, "I've been thinking about this. We need to trust her. She'll do the right thing. She'll be here."

Gomez sighed. "I hope you're right," he said. But Wednesday wasn't the only child he was worried about. Pugsley's practice sessions had gone from bad to worse over the last month. He had no idea how the boy was going to get through his Sabre Mazurka today without falling on his face, and as if that weren't bad enough, Pugsley's performance was going to be judged by none other than Great Aunt Sloom . . .

. . . Who was even now flouncing up the steps toward Gomez and Morticia. Gomez smiled his biggest, sweetest smile and swept forward to kiss her cheeks.

"Auntie Sloom!" he said. "You're as radiant as a barrel of nuclear waste!"

Sloom swept right past him. "Where's the boy," she demanded without turning her head.

"Pugsley?" Gomez asked nervously. He looked around and spotted his son. He was hanging from the chandelier.

"Oh, there you are," Gomez said heartily. "Come down and say hello to your Auntie Sloom!"

Pugsley attempted a graceful dismount but missed his mark and landed with a splat at Sloom's feet.

Sloom looked down at him as though he were a centipede waiting to be squashed.

"This better be good," she said. Then she swept away.

Pugsley looked up and caught Gomez's eyes. The two of them stared at each other in mutual panic.

This wasn't going to be good.

"Home is where the heart is!" Margaux Needler screeched into a bullhorn from her perch on the hood of a golf cart. The townspeople of Eastfield Estates, summoned by Neighborhood Peeps, had gathered in the town square. They listened angrily, yelling their agreement.

"If your *home* is awful, then your *heart* will be awful too!" Margaux went on. "I mean, that's just *math*!"

"Yeah!" someone in the crowd yelled. "Math!"

"We cannot allow these so-called *people* to ruin our neighborhood!" Margaux shrieked. "And destroy our property values!"

"It's not fair!" someone hollered. "We follow the rules! Why don't they have to?"

"I have *tried* reasoning with them," Margaux went on. "But they won't listen to me. They won't listen to Margaux!

Can you imagine?!"

"We listen to you!" someone else yelled. "Why don't they have to?"

"Well," Margaux hissed, "their time is up. We'll be revealing Eastfield Estates and all of you good people to our devoted viewership in just an hour! Our last chance to *help* these people—these, these *Addamses*—is now."

She leapt down from her golf cart and threw her fist into the air. "So follow me for some good old-fashioned Design Intervention! Bill—!" She gestured at a suburban dad. "John!" She pointed at another dad. "Do you have that lovely trebuchet you built in your woodworking club?"

Bill and John nodded grimly. "Yes, we do," they said.

The mob roared.

Glenn looked around him at the slavering mob. Then he looked at Margaux. She had a bloodthirsty light in her eyes. She'd clearly gone around the bend, and although Glenn figured it would make for good reality television, he wasn't sure if it was good for *reality*.

"Are you sure about this?" he asked Margaux. But she only screamed a bloodcurdling cry in response.

Up in the attic of Margaux Needler's house, Wednesday Addams and Parker Needler looked out the window and watched Margaux lead a crowd of unhinged townspeople up the hill toward the Addamses' house.

Wednesday turned to Parker, her face resolute. "Nobody torments my family but me," she said. She held out a hand, palm up. "Hair clip, please."

Parker looked confused. But she handed Wednesday a hair clip.

Wednesday knelt by the door and carefully slotted the hair clip into the keyhole. She pressed her ear to the door next to the lock and jiggled the hair clip just so, until—

Click!

The door sprang open.

"Cage School 101," Wednesday explained. "There are certain benefits to an unorthodox education."

Up at the unsuspecting Addamses' house, the celebration was in full swing. Thing carried a tray of hors d'oeuvres from room to room. It held a group of relations rapt with a fascinating tale. The shrunken heads sang their shrunken hearts out. And Auntie Sloom held court in the parlor.

"Sloom," Grandma Addams said affectionately, "you look *miserable*."

Sloom nodded archly. "Why, thank you," she said. "I've just returned from holiday."

"Where were you?" Grandma asked.

"The morgue," Sloom replied.

Morticia stepped up with a pitcher of cloudy, fetid liquid. "Auntie Sloom, can I get you another glass of dregs?" she asked, proffering the pitcher.

Sloom glared at her. "When's the Mazurka?" she demanded.

Morticia looked around nervously. "Soon," she said. "Soon. Our daughter Wednesday hasn't arrived yet."

Sloom sniffed. "That's not my concern," she said sharply.

Morticia straightened up. "Very well," she said. She looked across the room and caught Gomez's eye. She nodded.

Gomez took a deep breath. Then he raised his glass and clinked it loudly with a spoon.

"Attention, please," he said, clinking away, "Attention!" He clinked and clinked, then clinked so hard that the glass exploded in his hand. Finally, the crowd quieted down, and everyone turned to look expectantly at Gomez.

"The hour is upon us," he said. "Places!"

The entire congregated Addams and Frump clans trooped into the ballroom. Auntie Sloom climbed onto her special perch that had been set up for her at the head of the room and stared down imperiously. Gomez stood at her feet and addressed the crowd.

"We gather today to witness my son, Pugsley Addams, perform his Sabre Mazurka. He will begin with a reading from *The Terror*, which commemorates our Addams Family battle cries."

Pugsley walked shakily to the podium that had been set up for him. It flipped a huge tome open to the correct page, and Pugsley stood up at the podium. He looked solemnly down at the page, and then took a deep breath and opened his mouth.

"*YeaaaaaaAAAAAaaaaaAAAAAaaaaaAAAAAAgh!*" he shrieked. It was a sound of pure terror.

Gomez and Morticia exchanged glances again. Gomez winced. The terror in that scream had sounded a little too real.

At the podium, Pugsley moved on to the next portion of the ceremony. He closed his eyes, clenched his hands into fists, held his breath, and turned bright red. Just when it looked like he might pass out or suffer a brain aneurysm, his face exploded into a forest of facial hair.

The crowd erupted into cheers. Gomez beamed, tears springing from his eyes. So far, so good! The newly bearded Pugsley beamed out at the crowd, his triumphant grin almost completely hidden by the dense whiskers that had suddenly sprouted all over his face.

Fester stepped up, slinging a reassuring arm around Pugsley, and said in a booming voice:

"And now . . . the *Sabre Mazurka*!"

The lights went out, leaving the room pitch-dark. For a long moment, nobody breathed, and the dense blackness was completely silent.

Then a single spotlight clicked on, revealing Pugsley standing in the middle of the ballroom, very much alone.

Pugsley looked around him. He was half-blinded by the spotlight, but he could just make out, in the gloom surrounding him, all the many members of his very strange family. They were all looking at him. And then, on a cue, they all drew swords! Even Auntie Sloom. Still perched on her throne of judgment, she drew an impossibly long blade and pointed it directly at Pugsley. He swallowed hard.

Then his father emerged from the dark, bearing the ceremonial sabre. He pointed the sword at his son and said, very softly, "Hold still."

Pugsley held very, very still. Gomez took a deep, steadying breath, and then—*swish! swish! swish!*—the blade kissed Pugsley's bearded face three times.

Gomez stepped back, lowering the sword. The last

tufts of Pugsley's beard drifted down and landed silently on the floor. Pugsley raised a hand and ran it over his face. It was bare again, except for a small, dapper mustache that sat neatly on his upper lip.

The Addams mustache.

Gomez nodded, satisfied. "Now you are ready," he said to his son. He held the sabre out in two hands, and Pugsley reached a trembling hand out and took it.

It was time for the Sabre Mazurka.

Lurch began playing the music on the organ. Pugsley closed his eyes. Then he opened them, and the dance began.

Around him, members of his family began whirling and swaying to the music, brandishing swords. They swept in toward Pugsley, and before he could move—either to dance or to dodge—someone caught him with an elbow to the gut. He went down with an *oof*.

Pugsley scrambled up just in time to duck as a third cousin twice removed swept a sword at his neck. He scrambled toward the wall in a panic.

Suddenly, his father was there.

"Pugsley?" he said softly. Lurch stopped playing, and everyone in the room gasped in shock. They all slowly lowered their swords, confused.

"I give up," Pugsley said miserably.

A loud murmuring started up among the assembled Addamses. Pugsley looked around. His entire family had gathered from all over the world . . . just to watch him fail. He hung his head. He'd never felt so ashamed.

Gomez knelt down and looked up into Pugsley's face. Pugsley looked at his father, expecting him to look angry, disappointed, humiliated . . . but all he looked was worried.

"I can't do it, Pop," Pugsley said. He sniffled again and rubbed his nose on his sleeve. "I'm sorry I let you down."

"You haven't let me down, Pugsley," Gomez said. He looked into his son's eyes. "I've let *you* down. I was so focused on doing this the traditional way, I forgot to let you be who you are."

KRRRRRASH!

At that moment, a boulder crashed through the wall.

Everyone turned and looked out the hole in the wall to the lawn outside, where Margaux was standing on top of a golf cart, surrounded by furious townspeople. Next to her was an armed catapult. It was loaded with an enormous boulder, and there was a pile of huge stones next to it, waiting.

"*Hey, are you ready for your Margaux Makeover now?*" Margaux shouted into her bullhorn.

"For Hades's sake, not again!" Morticia said. "Margaux has turned the whole town into raving lunatics."

Gomez nodded. "I have to admit," he said, "I admire her work."

Margaux pulled the lever on the catapult, and a second boulder flew through the air and slammed into the house. *WHAM*.

Addams family members scattered, screaming, as the boulder crashed through the house.

"*GETTTTTTTTT OUTTTTTTT!*" cried the poltergeist. It fled the house and plunged into the remains of the swamp at the foot of the hill. The swamp water hissed and bubbled.

CHAPTER 9

Gomez pulled Pugsley tight. He was about to say something when Thing appeared out of nowhere, carrying a small mine—just the very kind of mine that Pugsley had been sling-shooting at his father a few weeks ago. Pugsley sighed just looking at it. It had been a more innocent time. A time of explosives and mayhem. A time when he knew what he was good at. A time before the Mazurka had ruined his life, and before a crazy woman from television had started knocking holes in his house.

Thing waved the mine at them again, and Gomez

gasped. Thing tossed Gomez the mine, and he snatched it out of the air.

"Pugsley!" Gomez said excitedly. "What is the Mazurka *about*?"

"It's about protecting our family from people who threaten our very existence," Pugsley said, confused. Why was his father asking him this *now*?

Gomez cocked an eyebrow and tossed Pugsley the mine. Pugsley caught it, and suddenly he understood.

Gomez grinned at Pugsley. "Go ahead," he said. "Show 'em what you're good at!"

Pugsley grabbed a baseball bat and batted the mine at an incoming boulder.

BLAM! The mine hit the boulder and blasted it into harmless dust before it could reach the house.

BLAM! The next boulder came flying, and this time Pugsley's mine broke it into shards. One of them flew into the wall, decapitating a portrait of a gloomy young woman. In the hole in the wall where her head had been, a different head popped up.

"Hey, guys!" cameraman Mitch piped up cheerfully. Margaux did a double-take. Had he been there ever since he vanished during their first tour of the house?

She shook her head. It didn't matter.

Fwip! The lever released the line, and the catapult flung another boulder at the house.

BLAM! Another perfectly thrown mine shattered it before it could wreck anything—or hit anyone.

BLAM! BLAM! BLAM! Margaux reloaded faster this time, but Pugsley was just getting started. Moving with grace and style, he executed the best Mazurka the family had ever seen, all the while flinging explosives at the boulders. The family clapped and cheered, and Pugsley laughed as he danced. He'd been born to do this! It was effortless, beautiful, joyful.

At least . . . until he ran out of mines.

Pugsley stopped dancing, patting his pockets furiously in case he had one socked away somewhere.

"Pop, I'm out of ammo!" he cried.

"We're trapped!" Gomez said, looking around. Piles of rubble penned the Addamses in. There was nowhere to run.

Margaux loaded another boulder into the catapult, laughing and laughing.

"Margaux Needler never quits a remodel until the project is *complete*," she said, aiming her boulder at the structural column on the east side of the house. Once that column was destroyed, the ceiling would fall, smooshing everyone inside the house. And that would be the end of the Addamses in Eastfield.

Pugsley, Morticia, and Gomez huddled together, watching helplessly. Everything they'd fought for . . . the strange, horrible, lovable home they'd made for themselves . . . the promise of a new land for their entire family . . . it was all about to fall to pieces, and there was nothing they could do about it.

KABOOM. The boulder crashed through, and the ceiling began—almost as though in slow motion—to fall.

And then it stopped.

Pugsley opened his eyes and peered up.

Ichabod the tree had caught the ceiling and was holding it in its branches. Wednesday sat primly on one of them, directing the tree's action.

"Ichabod, quick!" she said, pointing imperiously. The tree nudged the column back into place and gently set the ceiling back. Then it lowered one of its branches to the assembled Addamses. They all scrambled up the branch into the safety of the tree.

Down on the lawn, Margaux directed her suburban-dad henchmen to load one last boulder into the catapult.

"Here's a *boulder* design statement," she shrieked. Her hand hovered over the lever.

Snap! The soft but distinctive sound of fingers snapping caught Pugsley's attention. He looked up in time to see Thing fling one last mine in his direction. Pugsley snatched it out of the air, leapt off the tree branch, and landed with a flourish, slamming the mine against the catapult. The catapult exploded into a pile of wood chips.

"Mazurka!" Pugsley cried as he landed on one knee, his chest out and arms up. He raised his chin triumphantly.

There was a moment of silence, and then the assembled Addams and Frump clans went absolutely bonkers, cheering and clapping—and many of them hugging each other and openly weeping.

Wednesday hopped down from the tree.

Morticia reached out and gathered her in for a tender hug. "My little raven," she said, "I'm so proud of you."

The extended family continued to clap and cheer for a long while. But eventually they came back to themselves and remembered what had prompted the explosive Mazurka in the first place.

They turned to regard Margaux Needler and her mob of angry townspeople, only to discover that the townspeople weren't so angry anymore.

The people of Eastfield looked around themselves in total silence. Those who had been carrying pitchforks and shovels lowered them. A few of them started walking away, shaking their heads in confusion and disgust.

"They're not monsters . . ." one villager said.

"They're *family*," said another.

More and more of the townspeople began walking away.

"Oh, cry me a river!" Margaux yelled in outrage. "They *are* a bunch of monsters!"

She turned back to the Addamses. "Margaux Needler never stops until the project is complete!" she shrieked. "I will relish hounding you until that monstrosity you call a house is gone, and your mutant family with it!"

Morticia loomed over her. "Be careful what you wish for," she said icily. "My family and I will never run from the likes of you again."

Margaux snorted. "I'm outta here," she said, turning on her heel. "You can expect me when you least expect it, *Addams*." She gestured imperiously at Parker. "Parker! Let's go!"

But Parker didn't move, except to sidle closer to Wednesday. "I'm not going anywhere with you," she told her mother. "I'm staying with my friend."

"Your *friend*?!" Margaux said, whirling around in outrage. "Parker, these people are *freaks*."

Parker put her chin up defiantly. "If they're freaks," she said, "then so am I. And," she added, turning to the assembled townsfolk, "so are all of you."

Wednesday stepped forward. "Exhibit A," she said. "Ms. Gravely."

Ms. Gravely jumped a little bit, surprised to hear her name.

"You put your underwear in the freezer," Wednesday said.

"It's refreshing," Ms. Gravely answered, then blushed.

"Exhibit B," Wednesday said. "Trudy Pickering. You put ketchup on your birthday cake!"

"What?!" Trudy said. "That is—*how did you know that*?!"

"Because Margaux has hidden cameras in all your homes," Wednesday explained loudly, "and watches you *all the time*."

She turned to Margaux and smiled. "And that," she said, "makes you the freakiest of us all."

The crowd began to rumble angrily.

Margaux turned on them. "You're just a bunch of extras!" she shouted. "Who cares what you think? Now, if you'll excuse me, I have a live show to do."

She turned to go, but a voice stopped her in her tracks.

"Actually, Mom . . ." Parker said, and Margaux turned around slowly to see Parker walking toward her, phone held high.

"You've been live this whole time," Parker said.

Margaux went sheet-white.

"Three million people are watching you *right now*," Parker told her. She paused and glanced at her phone. "Wait," she added, "make that four million."

Brrring! Brrring!

A phone started ringing. Glenn grabbed his phone out of his pocket and slammed it up to his ear. He listened intently for a moment, then nodded.

"Margaux . . ."

Margaux whipped around. "*What*," she demanded.

"You're canceled," Glenn said.

CHAPTER 10

"Hello?" a voice piped up behind Morticia and Gomez. They turned to see Trudy Pickering looking at them nervously. She walked up, along with Mr. Flynn, a couple of dads, and a handful of other neighbors from Eastfield.

"I'm Trudy," Trudy said, holding her hand out to shake. "We've, uh, never officially met."

Morticia looked at her hand but didn't shake it. "The ketchup woman," she said coolly.

Trudy winced. ". . . Right," she said, lowering her hand

again. "Please," she said. "Just give us a chance to make it right."

Everyone turned to Morticia. Morticia said nothing. It was a very loud nothing.

Finally, Wednesday took her mother's hand and squeezed it. "Look," she said. "I've spent time with these people. And it's true, they *are* weird. But we shouldn't judge them just because they're different."

Morticia closed her eyes. Years—decades—centuries of persecution weighed down on her. But in the end, they were no match for the open-hearted appeal of her only daughter.

"I accept . . ." Morticia said, and held her hand out to Trudy. When Trudy took it, she discovered that shaking Morticia's hand was like shaking a dead fish.

". . . I suppose," Morticia added. She gave Trudy the tiniest of smiles.

If there was one thing that the residents of Eastfield had in common, it was a love of fleece jackets. If there was a second thing they had in common, it was a passion for home renovation. That very night, the entire town got to work on the project of repairing the Addamses' house. And the entire Addams and Frump clans pitched in.

By morning, the mansion was whole again. And by the end of the next day, every unoccupied home in East-field Estates had a new family in it—a Frump or Addams family.

EPILOGUE

Eastfield Estates was very different these days. On any given morning, you might see Thing walking Kitty on a leash through the town square. Or Uncle Onion tipping his hat to nearby townspeople. Or a gaggle of Eastfield Estates residents putting together a housewarming gift for a newly moved-in Addams.

All through Eastfield, old-timers mingled with their new Addams and Frump neighbors. Nowhere was there more mingling than in the local coffee shop, Assimilatte. The café was full to bursting every day as townspeople and Addamses gathered to chat, sip overpriced espresso drinks, and watch the world go by.

"One nonfat half-caf half-sweet almond milk mocha latte for Mildew!" Fester cried out. He'd taken a job as the new barista at the café, and he'd never been happier.

Margaux Needler looked around. Nobody else stood up to claim the drink, so she figured that probably meant that "Mildew" was "Margaux." She worked her way over to the bar and collected the cup.

"Here's your coffee, Ggerri," she said, handing the cup up to the horrible little man who had taken up residence in her hair. "Thanks, Mildew," he said.

Margaux shuddered. "My life . . ." she moaned.

Parker grinned. "Can you blame him, Mom?" she asked. "I mean, who wouldn't want to live in your hair, am I right?"

That evening, at the newly repaired Addams house, the doorbell rang.

Lurch lumbered over to the front door and opened it.

"You raaaaaang?" he moaned, looking out. There was nobody visible on the porch. But a shadowy rippling wave of air rushed into the house with an angry moan. The poltergeist was back. And as it swept through the house, all the nice new flourishes the townsfolk had added began to rust and drip. Mold appeared in the corners, and spider-webs wove themselves from the ceilings.

"*GETTTTTTTTT OUTTTTTTT!!*" the poltergeist shouted. Gomez and Morticia looked up from where they were gathered in the ballroom with some of their extended family.

"Oh, how lovely," Morticia said. "The spirit's home."

"Finally back to normal," Gomez agreed.

Auntie Sloom cleared her throat impatiently, and everyone turned back to her. She lifted her chin and continued the ceremony.

Pugsley approached Auntie Sloom slowly and solemnly. She placed a shako on his head.

"Pugsley," she said. "You are an Addams through and through."

The entire room erupted into cheers. Pugsley grinned, and even Wednesday cracked a smile.

"We did good," Gomez murmured.

Morticia smiled her unknowable smile. "I won't tell anyone if you don't," she said.